CW00429234

A HEART FULL OF SECRETS

HEART OF THE HILLS: BOOK ONE

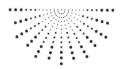

POPPY PENNINGTON-SMITH

First published 2021 by Bewick Press Ltd.

BEWICK PRESS LTD, JANUARY 2021
Copyright © 2021 Poppy Pennington-Smith.

This is a work of fiction. Names, characters, places and incidents either are the product of imagination or are used fictitiously. Any resemblance to actual persons, living or dead, events or locales, is entirely coincidental.

All rights reserved. Published in the United Kingdom by Bewick Press Ltd. This book or any portion thereof may not be reproduced or used in any manner whatsoever without the express written permission of the publisher except for the use of brief quotations in a book review.

www.bewickpress.com
www.poppypennington.com

1
ROSE

ROSE GOODWIN BLINKED into the pale morning light. She was sitting on the veranda, rocking gently in the porch swing with her feet dangling above the wooden decking below. It was early. She had wrapped a scarf around her shoulders, but the air was already humming with the promise of a warm day ahead.

Nudging a flyaway strand of hair behind her ear, Rose turned her face towards the sun. Climbing slowly over the Tuscan hills, its buttery hue was kissing the tops of the Cyprus trees in the distance and had painted the landscape a vibrant mixture of golds and greens.

Finally, Rose allowed her feet to touch the ground. They were bare – something she would have tutted at her children for, even though they were all grown up. But lately, stepping outside with naked feet each morning had become something of a habit.

Since she moved to *Heart of the Hills* ranch, over thirty

years ago, Rose had watched the sun glide up over this picturesque Italian vista too many times to count. Usually with her husband, Thomas.

Thomas was the reason she'd spent the best part of her adult life living in Italy amongst sunshine and horses instead of in England where she grew up. Had she not fallen in love with him, she could quite conceivably have spent the last three decades watching globules of rain slide down the grimy windows of her old accountancy firm's red brick offices. Unfulfilled. Unappreciated.

But she did; she fell head over heels for young British ranch owner Thomas Goodwin. And now, here she was – sixty-four years old, watching the place where they had lived, and loved, and worked alongside one another, blink its sleepy eyes and start a new day.

Sitting proudly on the crown of a hill, Rose and Thomas' ranch was surrounded by fields, winding streams, and small clusters of woodland. From the veranda of the main house, Rose could see the guests' cabins, the neat Italian gardens, the swimming pool, and the stables. Sometimes, on a clear day, she could almost make out the ocean on the horizon. But this morning, it was too hazy.

Loosening her scarf, Rose tried to shift her thoughts away from Thomas; today, of all days, she needed *not* to think of him. But, as always, once she'd started remembering, it was hard to stop.

When they first met, when they were still nervously side-stepping around one another and trying to hide their feelings, when Rose was simply a guest at the ranch and Thomas was her best friend's handsome older brother, he had brought her coffee every morning in a small blue takeout flask. They had sat beside one another and watched the day begin. They'd talked endlessly and made all kinds of plans. And when they got married, the tradition had continued.

For over thirty years, they had started each day together, side by side, with flasks of coffee. And Rose had always felt it was like pressing a reset button; a chance to start the day fresh, put aside any petty disagreements, and be thankful for their wonderful home and their beautiful family.

But eighteen months ago, Thomas had stopped coming outside with her.

It was late in February and he had been breaking in a new filly. Rose hadn't particularly wanted to take the young horse on, but Thomas had insisted; he loved a challenge, and something about Andante had spoken to him. He'd been making progress, but on their first trek in the hills beyond the ranch, something spooked her. Andante bolted. Thomas fell. And nothing was ever the same again.

That day, Thomas fractured several ribs, shattered his pelvis, and dislocated his shoulder. The doctors told him he'd probably never ride again. He was consumed by pain and sadness, and the husband Rose knew disappeared. Almost overnight, Thomas became a shadow of the man she fell in love with – a ghost who floated from room to room in the ranch house, refusing to set foot outside or allow anyone to help him.

Rose tried everything. She hired a first-class physiotherapist, then a first-class psychotherapist. She left him alone. She smothered him. She called the children who, one-by-one, came home to see if they could help. But nothing worked.

Thomas pushed them all away, and eventually, the children left again.

Catherine, the eldest, moved back into her apartment in the village nearby, Amelie returned to London and her publishing job, and the older of Rose and Thomas' twin boys, Ethan, flew home to New York. Only Ben, the younger twin, stayed to help. But even he couldn't make his father see sense.

Rose had been on the verge of calling in her last hope – her best friend, and Thomas' sister, Katie – when, six months ago, she woke one morning to find him gone.

At the turn of the new year, Thomas had packed his things in the dead of the night, snuck out of the ranch house, taken the car, and disappeared, leaving only two things behind; a pile of credit card debts and a note that said, '*I'm sorry. Please forgive me.*'

Now, six long months after she learned that Thomas had coped with the pain and anguish of his injury by racking up eye-watering gambling debts, Rose began each day alone. And she wasn't even close to getting used to it.

Rose scratched her index finger over a loose thread in the front of the embroidered cushion she was holding. She wasn't sure when she'd picked up the habit of needing to have a cushion on her lap if ever she was sitting down, but she knew why she did it; it was comforting to have something to hold.

She looked at the date on her phone. It was nearing the end of August and, while the ranch was still functioning, the staff were being paid, and the horses were being looked after, the summer would soon be over. And as the high season came to an end, Rose was facing a very dark winter. After the expense of the accident itself, Thomas' debt repayments were crippling their finances and, no matter how hard she tried, she couldn't see a way out of the situation he'd left her in.

Scraping her fingers through her shoulder-length light brown hair, she closed her eyes. With them open, she couldn't help thinking about the many, many jobs that needed doing. The money that needed spending. Closed, at least she could pretend for a few minutes that everything was just as it used to be. She could feel the gentle swaying of the porch swing, listen to the staccato'd melody of the birds and crickets, and pretend that any minute now Thomas would stride out onto the porch and kiss her forehead.

"Mum?"

Rose slowly released her breath, paused, then opened her eyes. Her youngest son's tall, stocky frame and dark messy hair instantly made her smile. "Good morning, sweetheart." She patted the seat beside her and nudged up to let him sit down.

He was holding two mugs of coffee and handed her one. "Black, two sugars."

"Thank you, just what I needed."

"You sleep okay?" Ben raised his eyebrows at her as he took a sip from his mug.

Rose shrugged her shoulders. "Yeah. Okay."

"Excited?" He was watching her intently.

Her heart fluttered. Had she forgotten something?

"Amelie? When does her flight get in? Ten?"

Of course – Amelie. "Ten thirty, I think." Rose looked down into the depths of her coffee. "Actually, I was wondering whether you'd take the truck and collect your sister for me?"

She hated lying to her children. But she couldn't tell Ben that she wanted him out of the way because she had an important appointment to keep. An appointment she didn't want him, or his siblings, to know about unless it was absolutely necessary.

"Sure." Ben sat back and took another sip of his coffee. "How come?"

Rose tapped her fingernails on the side of her mug and looked out towards the field where the first horses were being led out for their morning exercise. "Oh, you know, I want to make her room look nice, pick up some food for tonight." Without looking at her son, she added, "Perhaps, on the way back from the airport, you could drop into the village and visit Catherine? Check that she's still coming to dinner? I told her Amelie's flight gets in later, so it'll be a nice surprise."

Unaware that she was watching him, Ben rolled his eyes, but said, "Sure. I can do that." Ben and Cat had always gotten along just fine, but lately he was becoming increasingly frustrated with her. She worked at a tiny gelato shop, doing a job that she neither liked nor disliked, which paid very little and had no real prospect of becoming anything serious. For over a year, she'd been dating her boss. Which had no prospect of becoming anything serious. Everyone knew it was a bad idea, but Catherine refused to listen. And Ben was getting tired of being a sounding board for his sister's problems.

"At least with Amelie back home, she can take the heat

off you for a bit." Rose nudged Ben gently in the ribs and he laughed.

"Ha. Yeah. Right. Amelie won't be sympathetic enough."

"Well, maybe you should stop being sympathetic too? And then Cat will stop bugging you to listen to her." Rose raised her eyebrows. She knew Ben wouldn't do that; he was too sweet and loved his sister too much to tell her to shut up.

"You think she'd pay any attention to me if I told her what I really think?"

"Probably not."

"Exactly." Ben laughed again and shook his head; he pretended to hate it, but Rose knew that he'd do anything for his sisters. It was the thing she was most proud of in the world. Of course, she was proud of what she and Thomas had achieved with the ranch, and of leaving England and starting a new life in Italy. But, more than anything, she was proud of her children. Proud that they loved one another so much.

Rose vividly remembered the day she and Thomas had been told they were unlikely to conceive. It had broken their hearts, but then they'd decided to adopt and everything had shifted into place again. After a protracted process, not helped by the fact they were British and living in Italy, they finally adopted Catherine – six years old and cute as a button – then four-year-old Amelie two years later. With the girls, they felt like their family was complete. But then a miracle happened; Rose fell pregnant with twins. Ethan and Ben were born seven minutes apart – Ethan first, which he loved to remind his brother about – and suddenly they were a family of six.

Rose and Thomas Goodwin, and their four amazing children.

Except, now, it was just Rose Goodwin. And two of her four children were living hundreds of miles away.

Rose tried to dislodge the aching that settled in her chest whenever she thought about Ethan being in New York or Amelie being in London. In just a few hours, Amelie would arrive back in Italy. She'd be staying at the ranch for four entire weeks, the longest she'd been home since she moved away after college, and Ethan would be close behind her.

"Do you think you're ready?" Rose's lips crinkled as she pictured Ben trying to cope with both of his sisters in wedding mode.

"Ready?"

"I'm betting Amelie will have a few jobs lined up for you to help prepare for the wedding."

Ben made a grunting sound that reminded her of the noise he used to make when she woke him for school – disgruntled but resigned to what was about to happen. "I don't think I could ever be ready for Amelie and Catherine in the run up to a wedding." He slurped down the rest of his coffee, then balanced his empty mug on the arm of the porch swing. "It's going to be stupidly extravagant, isn't it?"

Rose shrugged. When anyone mentioned Amelie's wedding and how much money it might be costing, it brought a whisper of nausea to her throat. "Well, your sister moves in different circles these days. There are… expectations."

"Mmmm."

Rose patted her son's leg. "Jed's paying for it. He said that whatever she wants, he'll provide. So…"

"So, it's going to be marquees, fancy photographers, and designer suits?"

So far, Rose knew little about the arrangements except that the ceremony would be in the local church and that the reception would be at the ranch itself. She had offered to pitch in and help organise things, but Amelie had insisted she could manage. "She might surprise us," Rose said. "Maybe they've decided to keep it low-key?" She paused. Ben did too. Then, together, they burst into a thunderclap of laughter. Of course, it wouldn't be low-key; *low-key* wasn't in Amelie and Jed's vocabulary.

2
AMELIE

Amelie Goodwin took one last look at her sleeping fiancé. Trying not to notice the throb of nervousness in her stomach, she picked up her luggage and left a note on the console table in the hall – right beside the ornamental bowl that Jed unwaveringly deposited his keys in each evening – so he'd be sure not to miss it when he left for work in a few hours' time.

Love you. See you in a few weeks. Am xxx

As she closed the front door behind her, she blinked at the too-bright lights of the lobby. Their London apartment was small but expensive, on the top floor of a complex that had its own swimming pool, gym, and night porters. Down in the foyer, waiting for the taxi she'd ordered the night before, Amelie yawned sleepily and pushed her strawberry blonde hair from her face.

Usually, if she woke at this time, it was because she had a

breakfast meeting to prepare for and was too anxious to sleep. But all of that was over now; less than twenty-four hours ago, she had said goodbye to her executive desk, packed her possessions into a cardboard box, and plastered a smile on her face as she left her office for the very last time.

Flying home to Italy to get married was supposed to feel like a celebration – of new chapters, fresh starts, and exciting things to come. But when she woke that morning, her phone vibrating silently beneath her pillow, there had been a wedge of uncertainty in the pit of her stomach. And it wasn't going away.

Now, in the back of the taxi, watching the sun rise over London as they crossed Tower Bridge, that niggle was becoming problematic. Her heart was beating loudly – at least, it felt like it was – and her cheeks were flushed.

Amelie tried to slow her breathing and focus on what was waiting for her when she landed in Tuscany – her mum, her siblings, and the family's beautiful ranch. It was eight long months since she'd last visited, and she was desperate to see them. But while she couldn't wait to hug her mum, go riding with her brothers, and sit on the veranda drinking nutmeg tea with her sister, there was something she needed to tell them. And she wasn't sure how.

Last year, at just twenty-nine years old, and after working her way up the ladder ever since she left university, Amelie had secured her dream job; Commissioning Editor for the women's fiction imprint at one of London's biggest publishing houses. She loved it. All day long, she was surrounded by authors and books, and there were whisperings that she could be a director one day. But a few weeks ago, she had decided to give it all up.

When Jed had first tentatively suggested the idea over dinner one night, Amelie had balked at it; she'd worked long and hard to get where she was and couldn't quite believe that he'd expect her to press 'stop' on her career just because they were getting married. But then he'd mentioned starting a family, and Amelie had remembered her own upbringing. After a rocky start, she'd been adopted by two of the most incredible people in the world. And her childhood on a small Italian ranch in the Tuscan hills had been, frankly, idyllic. She wanted some of that for her own children. She didn't want to work long hours. She didn't want to hire a nanny or send her children to boarding school. And, although she and Jed weren't even going to start trying for a baby until after the wedding, she'd slowly gotten used to the idea of being a homemaker.

"Besides," Jed had whispered as he slung his arm around her shoulders on the sofa one evening, "haven't you always wanted to write a novel of your own? If you stay home, you can." Turning to her, he had looked into her eyes and smiled – the same devastating smile that had caught her off guard when they very first met. "I want to take care of you, Amelie. Let me take care of you..."

As she recalled the memory, Amelie closed her eyes and leaned her forehead against the cool glass windowpane in the back of the taxi. Jed was the kind of guy she'd always wanted – self-assured, handsome, and successful. Yet, dependable, and excited by the prospect of settling down and becoming a father.

At least, she thought it excited him. Until last night.

Over the past few weeks, as her workload had decreased, Amelie had been spending her free time looking up various sized properties for sale in the countryside surrounding London. Their apartment was wonderful, but it wasn't the right place to bring up a child. And, last night, as she waved goodbye to her colleagues, she had left the office determined to sit down with Jed and go through some of the options; if they saw something they liked, he could take a look while she was out in Italy preparing for the wedding. If it felt right, he could put in an offer, and they could have a new home waiting for them by the time they returned from their honeymoon.

When she'd arrived back at the apartment, however, it had been empty.

An hour later, Amelie had been in the bedroom, sulkily changing into a pair of joggers and a soft white t-shirt, when she finally heard Jed's keys in the front door. Padding softly into the hallway, she had smiled and leaned against the door-frame, her frustration already softening. But then she'd heard voices.

Frowning and pulling her long grey cardigan a little closer over her chest, she had straightened up. As the door opened, Jed's booming laugh had filtered in through the gap. And then he'd appeared, grinning and shaking his head at someone Amelie didn't recognise.

When Jed saw her, he stopped, glanced at the man beside him, then smoothly – as if she wasn't standing there in scruffy leisure-wear – said, "Hey, babe. This is Charles. A friend from work. We just landed a big new account and have some stuff to go over, but it shouldn't take long."

Amelie bristled as she remembered the nickname. *Babe.* He never called her that, which meant that 'Charles from work' was someone Jed wanted to impress.

To his credit, Charles had politely walked over and shaken Amelie's hand, blushing a little and rubbing the back of his neck as he said, "It's lovely to meet you, Amelie. Jed has told me so much about you."

Amelie had raised an eyebrow at him – a trick she'd learned from her sister Cat when they were teenagers – and smiled. "You too." Then she'd turned to Jed. "Sweetheart, can I have a word?"

Jed had gestured for Charles to go on through to the lounge and followed Amelie to the bedroom where he sat down on the end of the bed and started loosening his tie. "I'm sorry, Am. I swear it won't take long."

"Jed, I have to leave for the airport at four a.m. I need an early night." She had softened her tone and stepped forward, slotting herself between his knees and looping her hands around his neck. "We won't see each other for three weeks. I wanted to talk…" She glanced towards the iPad, which now sat on top of one of her cases, brimming with potential new homes. "About houses and the wedding and–"

Jed had un-looped Amelie's hands, standing up and shuffling her backwards. Swiftly, he'd kissed her on the forehead, then smiled. "Well, the houses can wait. Can't they? You're going to be away for weeks and then we'll be heading off on honeymoon straight after the wedding. There's absolutely no point in looking at places tonight. In fact, I think we should probably wait until after Christmas. By the time we're back from Bali and everything has settled at work, it'll be approaching December. Which is a terrible time to think about moving house."

Amelie's jaw clenched as she replayed Jed's words on a loop in her head. They were making her skin feel hot and prickly. But last night, she'd been too dazed by them to formulate a proper response. Instead, she had simply folded her arms in front of her chest and said, "Jed. We can't keep putting it off. We said we'd start trying for a baby on our honeymoon. If it happens…"

But Jed had laughed and shaken his head at her. "Amelie," he'd replied in a firm voice. "The baby thing won't happen straight away. It never does. And to be honest, babies are a whole different discussion, aren't they?"

"A different discussion?" Amelie's entire body had stiffened – every muscle suddenly tense. She'd quit her job under the assumption that they would start a family as soon as possible and now babies were a 'discussion' they needed to have?

"We've talked about babies before, Jed. A lot. We said right from the beginning, right from when we got engaged, that we *both* wanted to start a family as soon as possible. That's why–"

Jed had almost been at the door when he turned back and lowered his voice. "Exactly. As soon as possible. Which means it needs to be the right time. There's no sense rushing it."

"The right time?"

Now on the outskirts of London, Amelie shifted uncomfortably and pulled her handbag onto her lap so she could wrap her arms around it and squeeze tightly. *The right time,* he'd said – as if they hadn't already decided that straight after the wedding was the right time.

She pictured him, fingers on the door handle, stopping and looking back at her. He was tall, movie star, make-you-swoon levels of handsome, and whenever he smiled at her, it turned her to jelly. "Amelie Goodwin, I love you," he'd said. "We're getting married. We've got our entire life to figure these things out, and we'll talk. I promise. When I'm finished with Charles, we'll order takeaway. And I'll whisper sweet nothings and tell you how lost I'm going to be without you by my side for the next few weeks. Okay?"

In the back seat of the taxi, Amelie scraped her fingers through her hair and sighed. As a sign for the airport came into view, she counted from one to ten then back again; the swirling uncertainty that had lodged in her gut when Jed said those words – *it needs to be the right time* – was still there. And it was getting stronger.

3
ROSE

As soon as Ben had clambered into the truck and started out for the airport, Rose returned to the house to tidy herself up. She'd started the day in scruffy jeans, a plaid shirt with a hole in its right sleeve, and her riding boots. Traditionally, she'd only helped out with the horses when they were short staffed. For years, she'd managed the guests and the admin, and ridden purely for pleasure. But since Thomas' accident, she'd been spending a few hours every morning down in the stables doing what he used to do – grooming, exercising, and mucking out stalls.

She didn't mind it and often smiled to herself as she remembered how nervous she'd been when she first arrived in Italy. When she first visited *Heart of the Hills,* she was terrified of horses. It had taken weeks for Thomas to persuade her to go near one, let alone learn to ride. Now, she couldn't imagine her life without them, and even the more laborious tasks were quite cathartic.

But time was precious. With a ranch full of guests, no Thomas, and no extra full-time staff this summer, there was so much else that needed doing, and today in particular she had somewhere to be.

Rose stopped at the top of the stairs. Since Thomas left, she'd taken to sleeping in Catherine's old room, and she hadn't been into the master bedroom for weeks. Sucking in a deep, shaky breath, she walked towards it and rested her fingers on the door handle. When she pushed it open, the lingering scent of Thomas' aftershave drifted towards her and she steadied herself on the doorframe. Memories of the two of them were everywhere in the house. But nowhere more than here.

The rocking chair where she'd nursed Ethan and Ben sat directly in front of her, positioned so it looked out of the large picture window which framed the fields, pool, and gardens at the front of the ranch house. It had belonged to *Heart of the Hills'* previous owner, and Thomas had spent hours sanding it down and repainting it before the twins were born.

Rose closed her eyes. She could see it so vividly – her younger self rocking gently in the chair with a baby boy cradled in the crook of each arm, Amelie and Catherine peering down at their pink, wrinkly brothers and frowning because they weren't nearly as exciting as the girls had expected them to be. And Thomas… standing proudly behind her with his soft, warm hands on her shoulders.

Rose swiped at her cheeks with the back of her hand and willed herself to blink away the tears that were falling defiantly from her eyes. She'd tried so hard to be angry with

Thomas. Some days, she managed it. But today she was wavering. And today, of all days, she needed Thomas out of her head.

Focussing on the task at hand, she strode towards the wardrobe. When she opened it, she ignored the gaping hole where her husband's clothes used to hang and sifted through her small selection of dresses. When she found her smart red tea dress – the one with the little white flowers and three-quarter-length sleeves – she nodded. That would do.

At ten-thirty, Rose brushed down the front of her dress and peered into the mirror in the entrance hall. A few silvery strands of hair had escaped from the neat braid that she'd tied at the base of her neck, so she tucked them back into place. Then she did one last check on the cleanliness of the kitchen and the living room and walked confidently out onto the porch just as a large black Mercedes pulled up in front of the house.

Rose held her hand up to shield her eyes, then waved as the car door opened. Her chest tightened nervously, but she tried to smile. Unfolding his well-over-six-foot frame from the driver's seat, Alec Anderson smiled back. He was dressed differently from the last time they'd met – smart trousers and a pale blue shirt instead of jeans and a t-shirt. And his once dark hair was now a salt and pepper grey, accompanied by a neatly trimmed beard.

Rose counted to five under her breath before descending

the steps to greet him. When she held out her hand, Alec clasped it tightly between his and kissed her cheek.

"Rose, it's been too long," he said in a smooth American accent.

"It certainly has." Rose took her hand back and gestured to the house. "Shall we go in? I can make coffee?"

"Absolutely." Alec followed her inside, past the empty reception desk where she'd hung a sign that asked guests to call her mobile if they needed assistance, across the flagstone hall, and into the large family kitchen at the back of the house.

Heading straight for the coffee machine, Rose flicked it on and started sifting through a selection of coloured foil capsules. "Strong, extra-strong, or decaf?" she asked.

"Extra-strong," Alec replied, walking towards the French doors that opened up onto the ranch's extensive vegetable garden. After standing for a moment with his fingers laced behind his back, he smiled. "What a beautiful kitchen. I think I've only ever seen the one Nonna uses."

Rose smiled too; everyone called the ranch's long serving chef *Nonna*. She'd been chief cook at *Heart of the Hills* for what seemed like forever and no one knew how old she was, although Rose suspected she must be approaching eighty-five at least. "After we had the children, we built onto the back of the house and created our own kitchen. Nonna prefers it that way – next door is *her* domain. And I'm under strict instructions never to set foot inside." Rose handed Alec a mug of steaming coffee and looked at the large oak dining table near the French doors. Biting back memories of the family dinners and birthdays which had been celebrated in that very spot, she placed one hand across her stomach and turned back to Alec.

"Too right," he said. "And I, for one, wouldn't want to mess with Nonna."

A crisp, almost-uncomfortable silence hung between them. Eventually, Rose cleared her throat and said, "So... how do we do this?"

Alec shrugged, offering a smile that made his cheeks dimple beneath his beard. "I'm not entirely sure. I've never purchased a ranch before."

"And I've never sold one," Rose replied. "But I guess, even though you know the place, I should show you around? It's been years since you were last here. You've looked at the accounts and the paperwork I sent over?"

Alec nodded. "I have." He looked briefly at the table. "Do you mind if we sit?"

"Of course." Rose slid into a chair opposite him and crossed then uncrossed her legs.

"Rose," Alec said, pushing his mug from one hand to the other. "I've looked at the information you sent. And, obviously, I'm pretty excited about all of this. But I've got to ask – why in the world do you want to sell up? The ranch is doing great. The business financials are strong, you've been fully booked every year for the last fifteen summers." Alec sat back in his chair as if he was waiting for her to reveal a horrible truth that she'd purposefully left out of her correspondence. Of course, there was something she'd neglected to tell him. But it wasn't anything that affected the viability of the business itself.

Rose exhaled slowly. "Alec, we've known each other a

long time. You and Della visited every summer for how long? Eight years? And I'd like to think we're friends. So, I'm going to be completely honest with you."

Alec was watching her carefully, clearly trying to interpret the worried expression on her face.

"It's our *personal* finances that aren't great."

"I see..."

"You know Thomas has moved out. And you know he had an accident a while ago that stopped him riding." She clenched her jaw and forced herself to continue. "What I didn't tell you is that he got into trouble after the accident. Gambling. *A lot* of gambling."

Alec pursed his lips as if he was trying to stop his face from making any kind of definitive expression.

"I'm struggling to make the repayments. Our savings were all but cleared out after the accident. Thomas needed a lot of private physio and we had to make alterations to the house..." She trailed off, remembering the days immediately after Thomas came home, when the ranch house became cluttered with wheelchair ramps and the study was converted to a bedroom so he didn't have to make it upstairs. "If we sell up now—"

"You'll be able to settle your debts and start fresh," Alec cut in, saving her from having to say it out loud.

Rose nodded solemnly.

"What about selling shares? You might not have to sell the *entire* business?"

"It..." Rose's mouth felt suddenly too dry, "it wouldn't be enough," she said quietly.

For a moment, Alec remained silent. But then he said, "And Thomas agrees with the sale?"

"Yes," she said. "He does."

Three hours later, Rose flopped into a chair outside *Signiorelli's* and waved through the window at the tall, dark-haired woman behind the counter. Waving back, Bea stuck her head out of the door. "Five minutes, *Piccola*."

Rose smiled. Her friend's thick mop of curls, lilting Italian accent, and always flushed cheeks never failed to lighten her mood. Although today, she had to admit; it was a struggle to feel anything but melancholy. "Okay," she mouthed as Bea ducked back inside.

Trying to relax the tension in her neck, Rose rubbed at it with her palm. In front of her, the village of *Legrezzia* was bustling with midday activity. A small village, with just a few grocery stores, Bea's café, and a twice-weekly market, it was only a ten-minute drive from the ranch and was becoming more and more popular with tourists looking for an out of the way bolthole.

Over by the fountain, Rose recognised a few guests from the ranch. But otherwise, the square was quiet, with just a few easy-to-spot locals here and there. It was warm, getting hotter, and approaching mid-morning. Rose looked at her watch. Amelie's flight would have landed by now and she'd be on her way to *Sant Anna* from the airport, probably talking Ben's ear off about the wedding.

Ben had promised to stop and visit Catherine on the way back, so Rose had a little while to spare before they all arrived at the house. Which was good; she needed to pull herself together. By the time the children hurtled through the front door and filled the rooms with long-overdue noise and energy, she needed to be *normal*. Or as close to normal as she could manage.

Finally, Bea emerged from inside holding two large glasses of red wine. She offered one to Rose and sat down beside her.

"It's a little early," Rose said, wrinkling her nose at the Italian wine she'd never quite gotten used to.

"You look like you need it," Bea said, tilting her head. "How did it go?"

"Alec is very interested."

"In the ranch? Or in you?" Bea raised an eyebrow as she sipped her wine.

"In the ranch."

"You can't blame me for asking."

Rose rolled her eyes. Alec and his wife Della had visited *Heart of the Hills* every summer for over eight years. Their son Skye was just a little older than Amelie, and the two of them had been thick as thieves. But one unexpected summer, just before the children turned sixteen, Alec had arrived at the ranch alone. He and Della had separated. So, Rose took him under her wing. She invited him to family dinners, let him help her with the horses, spent hours and hours listening to him talk about where he thought it had all gone wrong – in his life and in his marriage. And then on his very last evening before flying back to New York, Alec had tried to kiss her.

"Nothing ever happened between us, Bea, you know that."

"I know," her friend replied, smiling. "But he wanted it to."

"He was confused. He was missing Della. They got back together straight after he got home."

Bea shrugged, the way she always did when she had said something that she intended to leave floating in the air.

"He was devoted to her right up to when she died," Rose added solemnly.

"I'm sure he was. But he's been a widower for three years now, Rose. And you're..." Bea trailed off and swirled her wine around her glass.

"Alone?"

"Yes."

Rose leaned forward and rested her forearms on the table, pressing her fingertips together. "Alec is interested in the ranch. He has money. Lots of it. And if I have to sell, I'd rather it was to him than someone I don't know."

Quietly, Bea asked, "Do you have to sell? I mean, really?"

Rose stared at her wine glass before picking it up and drinking a too-large mouthful. "Yes, I think I do."

For a moment, the two of them sat in silence. Then Bea reached for Rose's hand and squeezed it gently. "I'm sorry."

"Me too."

After finishing her wine and leaving at least a third in the bottom of the glass, Rose waved goodbye to Bea and, from *Signiorelli's,* crossed the cobbled village plaza to the fountain. There, she dropped a coin into the water and made a wish.

As she watched the small gold disc slowly sink beneath the surface, she clasped her hands together tightly. "Please," she whispered, "help me do the right thing."

4
AMELIE

TAKING ANOTHER SIP OF CHAMPAGNE, and telling herself to stop overthinking everything, Amelie settled into her business class seat and flipped open the first in a large stack of bridal magazines that she'd purchased at the airport. She'd almost been swayed by the display of paperbacks at the front of the shop, but had reasoned that if she started reading a novel, she would slide unwittingly back into work mode. And she was supposed to be forgetting work.

She was folding down the corner of a page that featured a 'naked' cake, covered with berries and translucent icing instead of the traditional kind, and wondering whether it would be too late to call the caterers and change what she'd selected, when a commotion from further back in the cabin caused her to stop.

"I'm sorry, sir, economy passengers need to use the restrooms at the rear of the aircraft."

"I know that, ma'am, but this lady is very pregnant. One

of the restrooms is out of order and the large guy from aisle eight has been in the other one for fifteen minutes. Surely, you can make an exception?"

Amelie turned and peeked over the back of her chair. The stewardess was gripping the curtain that separated economy from the higher-paying passengers and shaking her head. "I'm sorry. Let me go down there and see what the hold-up is. Please, if both of you could return to your seats?"

The stewardess swished through the curtain and disappeared.

Rolling her eyes at the ridiculousness of not allowing a pregnant lady to use the bathroom just because she had an economy ticket, Amelie returned to her magazine. But a few moments later, movement in the aisle made her to look up.

As if he was trying to smuggle someone into Buckingham Palace, the man from economy was ushering a very heavily pregnant woman through the curtain and towards the business class bathroom. "I'll stand guard," he whispered conspiratorially in an American accent.

"Thank you," the woman mouthed, bobbing up and down on the balls of her feet before she squeezed herself into the cubicle and locked the door.

Amelie stifled a smile. In a window seat nearby, a grey-haired man in a suit was tutting and shaking his head but hadn't dared to say anything.

"Amelie?"

She glanced towards the restroom, confused by the sound of her name.

"Amelie Goodwin?"

Amelie narrowed her eyes, taking in the tall, dark-haired

man who had spoken to her. He was standing with his back to the restroom door – as if he was afraid the stewardess would return and haul his pregnant companion back out into the cabin before she'd finished peeing – and had a surprised but pleased expression on his face.

"Skye?" Amelie's mouth dropped open in surprise.

Smiling, the man stepped forward. He was older than the last time they were together, with a lightly stubbled jaw and thin lines at the corners of his sea-green eyes. But he was, undoubtedly, Skye Anderson – the American boy who had visited her family's ranch every summer for eight years. The American boy who she and Cat had both secretly swooned over. The American boy who...

"I can't believe it's you." Skye stepped forward a little. "How long has it been?"

Amelie hurried to her feet. She was grinning. She knew she was and yet, she couldn't seem to stop. "Too long," she said. "Far too long. We last saw each other... I don't know. Ten summers ago?"

Skye swept his fingers through his mop of dark curly hair, a gesture that exposed a small neat scar above his right temple. "Must be," he said, shaking his head. "You're heading home? To the ranch?"

Amelie was about to answer when, behind her, the air stewardess flounced back through the curtain and announced, "Sir. Please. I must ask you to return to your seat."

"Of course," Skye replied politely. But Amelie cut in.

"Come on. Really? His girlfriend is heavily pregnant. She's not doing anyone any harm, she just needs to pee."

"Miss Goodwin, I'm not trying to be difficult. I promise

you..." The stewardess looked sincere and apologetic, but Amelie wasn't going to give in; a sisterly sense of indignation was throbbing in her belly, and she was about to raise her voice when Skye said, "Oh, she's not my... we don't..." He laughed awkwardly and gestured back towards his seat. "We just met, and–"

"I'm sorry." Amelie shook her head. "I just assumed..."

Beside the window, the man who'd tutted stood up too and, ignoring Skye and Amelie, said to the stewardess, "Can you do something about this? Please?"

"Of course," she replied sweetly. But as she turned back to Amelie, the toilet door swung open and the pregnant woman emerged. She looked grey around the edges and was gripping the edge of the door.

"I'm sorry," she said, resting her other hand on her stomach. "Morning sickness seems to have returned with a vengeance."

"Oh, for goodness' sake," the man exhaled loudly, but Skye was already stepping forward to help the woman into the aisle.

Without thinking, Amelie bundled her magazines into her arms, grabbed her handbag, and said, "Here. Take my seat. Then you'll be right next to the bathroom if you need it."

"I couldn't..." The woman tried to protest, but Amelie nodded fervently. "Of course you can." She turned to smile at the air stewardess. "There's no rule against seat swapping, is there?"

"No. It's fine."

"Good." Amelie handed her new friend an unopened bottle

of water from the small table beside the seat and nodded at her. "Drink this, and I'm sure…" She peered at the stewardess' name badge. "I'm sure that Karen will take really good care of you."

"Thank you. So much." The woman smiled weakly. "I'm Rebecca, by the way."

Amelie shook Rebecca's hand and introduced herself, but then felt Skye tug at her elbow.

"We'd better make ourselves scarce," he whispered, nodding towards Window Seat Guy, whose face was almost puce with irritation. "Before he has a coronary."

As Amelie sat down beside Skye and heaved her stack of magazines onto her lap, he waved at the food cart that was heading towards them.

"Coffee?" he asked her.

Before she could stop herself, Amelie wrinkled her nose; she'd had airline coffee before, and it was always disappointing. "I might stick with tea."

"Right," Skye laughed. "I almost forgot that you're technically British and not Italian."

Amelie tilted her head from side to side and, in her best Italian accent, said, "Oh, I don't know. I think I'm a little of both, really."

Handing her a cardboard cup and a small sachet of milk, Skye smiled. "And your fiancé? Is he British?"

Amelie was about to take a sip of tea but stopped with the cup almost at her lips. "How did you…?"

"The ring and the magazines are a bit of a giveaway." Skye raised his eyebrows as he gestured to Amelie's lap.

"Ah. Of course." Instinctively, she pushed the magazines into the empty seat beside her and rolled her eyes at herself. "I'm not really a bridal magazine kind of person. These are the first I've read." She gave a small laugh then realised she hadn't answered Skye's question. "He's British. His name's Jed. He proposed just before Christmas." She didn't add that they'd only been dating for six months before Jed proposed – most people thought it was either terribly crazy or terribly romantic. And Amelie herself wasn't entirely sure anymore which one it was.

"Congratulations." Skye looked down at his own empty ring finger, then smiled at her. "So, you're going out to the ranch to see your parents?"

Amelie hesitated; she'd developed a habit of not really talking about her father. With most people, it was easy. But Skye's memory of the Goodwins was of how they used to be – a happy but chaotic family of six. Not five.

She cleared her throat and rested her cup on the tray table in front of her. "Mum, yeah. Cat and Ben are still there too. Ben and Ethan went out to New York to study medicine at Columbia, but Ben came home last summer. Not a fan of New York, apparently." Amelie was avoiding Skye's question. Eventually, like ripping off a plaster, she added, "My dad's not around anymore."

Skye's face dropped, and he reached for Amelie's arm.

She frowned at him, wondering whether he already knew what had happened, but then realised that he had interpreted her words very differently from how she'd meant them.

"Oh," she said. "No, he's fine. He's *around*, he's just not…"
She breathed in sharply through her nose. "Sorry. It's hard to
talk about. He had a riding accident about eighteen months
ago and then in January he just... left." For the first time in a
long time, Amelie felt like she might be about to cry and
blinked quickly. "He left my mum, and we don't know where
he is."

Skye hadn't taken his hand away from Amelie's arm and
now squeezed it gently. "I'm sorry, Amelie. I can't believe it.
Your dad – he's such a stand-up guy. And your parents were
always so…" He trailed off.

"Happy?"

"Yeah."

Amelie straightened her shoulders and moved her neck
from side-to-side. She was talking too much, feeling sorry for
herself, and Skye had been through a lot himself since they
last knew one another; his mother had died a few years ago.
Amelie remembered her parents telling her about it, and how
shocked she'd been. Skye's mother, Della, was the kind of
woman who lit up a room. Slim, blonde, and with a huge
pearly white smile, she had been so vivacious it was almost
impossible to imagine that she wasn't around anymore.

"Skye, I–" She was about to tell him that she was sorry
and ask how he was coping. But asking that kind of question
on a plane, surrounded by other people, when they hadn't
seen each other for almost a decade, felt… too much. "I
guess some things happen that we just can't control, though,
don't they?"

"They certainly do." Briefly, Skye reached up and let his
index finger trace the scar on his forehead. But then he

smiled and looked back at Amelie's magazines. "Still, good things on the horizon though?"

"Yes," she said, attempting to smile and to sound like a bride who was excited about her wedding. "In just a few weeks, actually. We're getting married at the end of August. At the ranch."

"August? Wow. That's soon."

He was right; it *was* soon. When Jed first proposed, they didn't talk about setting a date. But after her father disappeared, life had felt so fragile that Amelie didn't see the point in waiting. Jed hadn't even met her family, but when she suggested they get married at *Heart of the Hills* in the summer, he thought it was a splendid idea. So, just like that, Amelie called her mother and, probably because she was glad to have something to look forward to, Mum agreed.

Changing the subject, because thinking of everything she was going to have to organise in just four weeks made her feel a little woozy, Amelie tucked her hair behind her ear and asked, "What about you? I haven't even asked why you're on your way to Italy."

Taking out his phone and showing her a picture of him and his father, Alec, Skye smiled. "I'm meeting my dad. He's been working overseas a fair bit lately, I have too, so we thought we'd reconnect somewhere we both loved back in the day. We've got a rental place booked in *Sant Anna*. So, not far from you guys." He put his phone back down and took a long sip of coffee.

"You've been overseas?"

Skye sat back in his seat and, despite the limited room, crossed one leg over the other, balancing his ankle on his knee and jiggling his foot. "The forces," he said, a little more gruffly than she'd expected.

Amelie raised an eyebrow; she'd never pictured Skye as the army type.

As if he'd sensed her gut reaction, he said, "It's a long story. I studied veterinary medicine at UCD, met a guy who was in the Veterinary Corps…"

"I didn't even know the Veterinary Corps existed."

"Oh, sure," Skye said, his eyes brightening. But then he looked down at his hands and briefly closed his eyes. When he opened them, he cleared his throat. "But I'm not serving anymore. I'm now officially between jobs, so…" He waved his arms at the aeroplane cabin.

"So, you're taking a well-earned vacation?"

"Exactly."

Amelie bit her lower lip. It was the perfect opportunity; she could so easily have said, *How funny. I'm between jobs too.* She could have heard how it sounded and seen how Skye reacted before telling her family. But she didn't. She let the moment pass. And soon, after answering Skye's questions about London and filling him in on Cat's gelato store, and the mini feud between Ben and Ethan, the overhead tannoy announced that they were beginning their descent into Pisa Airport.

As she reached the bottom of the steps at the back of the plane, Amelie smiled. The Italian sunshine danced across her cheeks. It wasn't even mid-morning yet, and it was already warm.

Behind her, Skye was carrying a small hand-luggage sized suitcase, and he set it down as they reached the tarmac. "So," he said tentatively. "I know you're going to be busy the next few weeks, but if you have time for a coffee – or if you're visiting with Cat – maybe we could meet in *Sant Anna*?"

"You're not going to come up to the ranch?" She'd assumed that if Skye and Alec were in the area, they would visit *Heart of the Hills*.

Skye rubbed the back of his neck, and Amelie was almost certain that she saw him glance at her engagement ring. "I…"

"Mum would love to see you both. And I'd like a riding companion, if you're up for it – Cat's never been bothered with horses, and Mum and Ben will be busy with the guests. We could head down to the beach or do the river trail?"

Skye looked at her then smiled. "Sure. Okay. If you give me your number, I'll text, and we'll hook up."

Amelie blinked. Should she skim over his slightly awkward choice of phrasing or laugh at it?

Skye had paused too, and his cheeks were flushed. "I mean, get together for a ride. A trek." He exhaled loudly, making a horse-like sound with his lips. "Was I always this awkward? Because I feel as if I got awkward since we were kids."

"I think you probably were, actually," Amelie said, nudging his arm to show that she was teasing him. "But here…" As they began to walk towards the terminal building, she reached into her purse and took out one of her last remaining business cards – totally irrelevant now, except for her phone number at the bottom.

Skye took it, made an *impressed* face as he read her title, then slipped it into his back pocket. "Okay," he said purposefully. "I'll call you."

5
ROSE

BACK AT THE RANCH, Rose flicked on the radio and emptied the groceries from her wicker shopping basket onto the worktop. She'd bought fresh tomatoes, garlic, lemons, and spinach, but she would pick the oregano from Nonna's garden.

Despite all the fancy dishes she'd made over the years, the kids' favourite remained spaghetti with a rich tomato sauce. The secret, which Rose never told them, was the oregano. And just thinking of it made her smile.

Glancing at the large wooden dining table, her smile faltered. Was she really contemplating saying goodbye? Was she really on the verge of handing the ranch over to someone else?

"Rose?"

Nonna's deep Italian voice floated into the room and made her jump.

"You are away with the fairies," Nonna said, cupping Rose's face with her soft hands and smiling. "Is everything all right?"

Rose smiled back and shook her head, avoiding the question. "How was breakfast? Everyone's fed and watered?"

Nonna tilted her head from side to side. "Ah," she said, "it was *okay*. The guests were happy, but I am not convinced about the new hen. Her eggs are…" Nonna shrugged. "Not as good as Sicily's."

A month ago, Nonna had lost her favourite chicken, and she was *not* a fan of the bird's replacement. In her eyes, no hen would ever compare to Sicily – a plump white chicken who had served them faithfully for six years.

Rose patted Nonna's shoulder. "Give her time. She'll get there." Then she turned to the hob. "I'm going to make tea. Would you like some?"

Nonna tutted loudly. "I shall make it. You sit." But as they waited for the kettle to boil, Nonna suddenly threw up her hands and gasped.

Rose looked up to see the cook wielding a packet of spaghetti and waving it in the air. As if she'd discovered a stash of illegal drugs, Nonna shook the packet and said angrily, "Rose – what *is* this?"

Rose stifled a laugh. "Pasta. Don't worry, I bought the good kind."

"You are using this for what?" Nonna crossed her arms in front of her plump chest and narrowed her eyes.

"Dinner tonight. Amelie–"

"No. No, no, no." Nonna marched across the kitchen and,

rather dramatically, tossed the spaghetti into the rubbish bin. "The first time in – how long? The family will be together, and you want to feed them dried spaghetti from the shops? No. I will make it."

"Nonna, honestly," Rose breathed, getting up to retrieve the pasta. "It's fine. The kids won't know the difference."

Almost as soon as she'd spoken, she regretted it. Nonna placed a hand over her chest as if she was physically wounded and her face fell. "You're telling me they won't know *Nonna*'s pasta from something you bought from the shops?" She shook her head. "Nonsense."

"I promised them their favourite, and you're far too busy…"

"I will make some now. You can still…" Nonna wafted her hand over the small collection of ingredients on the countertop, "make the sauce. But I will make you *fresh* pasta." And before Rose could object, the short, rotund, determined old woman sploshed boiling water into a mug, added a tea bag and some milk then, leaving the world's weakest cup of tea on the kitchen table, hurried off to her own kitchen.

Alone with her tea, Rose sighed and took out the small black notebook she always kept in her handbag. Under a list titled, *To Ask New Owner*, she wrote: *Will they keep Nonna?*

Then, before she could begin to feel nostalgic, she tucked it away, turned up the radio, and thought of her children. Right now, they'd be on their way from the airport to the small town of *Sant Anna* where Catherine worked. She pictured Amelie and Ben singing along to a throw-back playlist from their teenage years or gossiping about Cat's love life, arms hanging from the open truck windows, smiles on their faces. And slowly, she felt lighter.

Looking around at her beloved kitchen, she exhaled a long, slow breath. Perhaps it really was time to move on.

6
AMELIE

"So, what's he like?" Ben was driving with one hand on the wheel and the other dangling out of the truck window. It made Amelie feel nervous, despite the fact that the roads were almost empty, and that Ben had driven this way for as long as she could remember. She resisted the urge to tell him to stop.

"Who?" She was leaning forward and repositioning the air vents so they were puffing cool but stale smelling air onto her cheeks.

"Your fiancé?" Ben laughed, as if it should have been obvious.

"Jed? Oh, he's…" Somehow, she couldn't think of the right words. Back home, whenever someone asked, she described Jed as 'erudite' or 'ambitious' or 'handsome'. But these were not words that would impress her brother. "He's great. You'll love him."

Ben glanced at her and nodded. "When's he flying out?"

"In a couple of weeks." Amelie looked down at her phone, surprised that Jed hadn't texted to see if she'd arrived safely. Sighing to release the unexplained tension in her chest, she sat back and wriggled her shoulders into the familiar soft leather of the passenger seat that she'd ridden in hundreds of times over the years. Looking out of the window, she added, "He's happy for me to finish up all the arrangements for the wedding. Apart from the drinks... the only thing he's stipulated is that we absolutely have to have some special kind of champagne from a vineyard up near Florence. Apparently, it's the best in the world. And he's invited a couple of important clients, so..." She shrugged, aware that she was making Jed sound a little too upper crust but unsure how to correct herself. "But apart from that, and the dress, and the food, pretty much everything's sorted, anyway."

"Is that all?" Ben was pinching his lips together, trying not to laugh.

"It'll be fine. All the appointments are lined up. It's wedding planning, not rocket science."

As she spoke, she caught herself wincing. She had noticed the plummy lilt to her voice, and it made her feel uncomfortable. Ben, of course, didn't react. He wouldn't, even if he'd picked up on it. But Amelie was suddenly very conscious of the fact that she was different from how she used to be.

She hadn't felt this way when she'd returned after her father's accident. Or when she came home for her mum's birthday last year. Perhaps it was seeing Skye that had unnerved her. Because he'd reminded her of how she was when they were kids.

"Have you heard from Dad?" Ben interrupted her train of thought, and the question surprised her.

"No." She angled herself so she was facing him and could examine his expression. "Have you?"

Ben's jaw twitched. "Not a word. But I think Ethan's in touch with him."

"Really?" Amelie's eyes widened; as far as she knew, none of her siblings had any desire to speak to their father.

Ben shuffled in his seat and Amelie watched an ever-so-slight pinkness flush his cheeks. "We rowed about it. I haven't told Mum."

"Oh," Amelie replied tentatively.

For twins, Ben and Ethan had always been remarkably different. They were inseparable. But they also grated on one another. Whenever Amelie thought of her childhood, it was full of lazy summer days when the boys would get into scrapes, fall out, declare they would never speak to one another again and inevitably – with encouragement from Amelie and Cat – reconcile.

For a while now, however, it had been apparent that their father's moonlight flit had driven a wider-than-before wedge between the boys. From the beginning, Ethan had been relatively nonchalant about the whole thing. As far as he was concerned, their father's depression and subsequent disappearing act was a minor blip in the family's timeline that would blow over. Dad needed time to get himself together but would return soon, and everyone should stop worrying about it. But Ben felt differently.

Until a year ago, Ben and Ethan had both been studying medicine at Columbia University in New York. Amelie had always found it amusing that, although they argued, the twins couldn't even contemplate being apart from one another. To the extent where, when Ethan decided he wanted to study in America, Ben unquestioningly followed suit.

After their father's accident, however, Ben returned home to help out for the summer and Ethan remained in New York. It was an unremarkable summer, but just before the autumn term was due to restart, Ben suddenly declared that he was going to stay in Italy. He dropped out of Columbia. And Ethan was devastated.

Amelie had received a call from him at four a.m. one morning. He was walking home from a bar and had just finished arguing with Ben by text message.

"He's adamant, Amelie. You've got to talk to him. He's throwing away his future. Two years of medicine and he's jacking it all in. For what?! And why isn't Mum doing anything about it?"

Blinking into the darkness of her apartment, and trying not to wake Jed, Amelie had padded through to the kitchen and flicked on the kettle. Putting her brother on speaker phone, she had rubbed at her eyes and, after letting him rant a little longer about Ben dropping out because he couldn't be bothered to work hard and using their father's behaviour as an excuse, she had finally stopped him. "Ethan... you miss him, don't you?"

On the other end of the phone, Ethan had gone quiet. Then, eventually, he replied. "Yes."

"And you're worried about him?"

Ethan cleared his throat. "I guess."

"Then stop being so pig-headed and tell him. Maybe if he knows how you feel, he'll change his mind."

But Ben didn't change his mind. He stayed at the ranch. And the twins' relationship had not yet recovered.

In the driver's seat, Ben drummed his fingers on the steering wheel. "I don't get it. I don't get why Ethan's on Dad's side in all this."

"Should we be taking sides?" Amelie asked cautiously.

"Probably not. But after what happened..." He trailed off. "Do you even know if he's coming to the wedding?"

Amelie blinked at the question. She'd been trying not to think about the fact that she was still carrying her father's wedding invitation in her handbag because she didn't know where to post it to. "Of course, he's coming." She bit the inside of her cheek. "He wouldn't miss my wedding, Ben. No way."

For the rest of the journey, Amelie remained silent. But as they drew closer to *Sant Anna* she let out a sigh that caused her brother to turn to her.

"You okay?" he asked, turning down the radio.

Amelie nodded; she didn't know why she felt suddenly tearful. "You know what I love about this area of Italy?"

"The olive oil?" Ben replied, smiling cheekily.

"The fact it never changes." Amelie looked out of the window and tucked her hair behind her ear. "Back in London, it seems like new buildings crop up every few days. There's always a new bar, a new shop, a new place to eat. But here…"

"It's the same as it was fifty years ago?"

"Pretty much."

Ben paused, and she wondered whether he was about to tell her to appreciate London for what it was – vibrant, exciting, exhilarating. But he didn't. "Yeah," he said, "change is overrated."

Soon, the car pulled onto a long winding road that climbed up between tall lusciously green Cyprus trees. The truck shuddered a little at the incline, and Amelie wriggled in her seat – the way they had as children when their parents had told them to help encourage the vehicle to make it up the slope. After a while, it levelled out, and they began the approach into the town.

Cat's gelato store was in the centre of a large plaza that attracted the bulk of the area's tourists, sandwiched between an expensive jewellery outlet and a popular restaurant. Out front, small round tables with yellow parasols were already bustling with customers, despite it still being early. Unable to drive into the plaza itself, Ben swung the truck down a far-too-small alleyway and parked on a residential street that, really, they should have had a permit for.

"No one ever checks," he said, noticing Amelie frown at him.

An anxious twinge niggled at her chest. Jed would *never* do something like that; he would break out in a cold sweat at just the thought of receiving a parking fine. But as she swung her legs out of the truck, she shrugged off the feeling and focussed on the comforting tap of her sandals on the cobbled floor.

"Did Mum tell her we were coming?" Amelie asked as they ducked into a small pedestrian passageway that led between two tall thin houses and back into the plaza.

"I don't think so," Ben mused. Then he grinned and put an arm around Amelie's shoulders. "She'll be psyched to see you."

The windows of the gelato store were tinted, so they couldn't see inside. Spotting a spare table beneath one of the parasols, Ben gestured for Amelie to sit.

"I'll go get her. Wait here."

And with that, he disappeared.

Sitting down in one of the light grey wicker chairs, Amelie looked up and smiled. The yellow parasol was the same colour as the buttercups that used to grow in the fields beyond the ranch. Gently, she touched her throat with her index finger.

"Do you like butter?" She remembered Skye, so many times, playing that game with her when they were kids – picking a buttercup and holding it beneath her chin to see if a tiny spot of yellow appeared on her pale skin. It always did. And she always refuted it. *"It's not true! I hate butter!"* she'd cry, to which he would shake his head and say, *"Nature never lies. And no one hates butter. That's just silly."*

"Ben, what is it? I'm in the middle of a shift." Her sister's voice nudged Amelie back into the present.

"Okay, well, just come out here for a second then. I have a surprise for you." Amelie could see Ben holding Cat's arm, and finally, she ducked beneath the parasol. Her hair was shorter, still a luscious dark shade of brown, and she was wearing her customary red splash of lipstick. Today, it matched her earrings.

Amelie waved. A small gesture that didn't even almost express the joy that was bursting in her chest at the sight of her sister's tall, beautiful frame.

Cat's mouth dropped open, and she put her hand in front of it. Then she looked at Ben. "You and Mum said her flight got in *tonight.*"

Ben shrugged. "We fibbed."

Amelie stood up but before she could reach out her arms, Cat had hurtled forward and was squeezing her so tightly that she thought her ribs might collapse.

"I don't think I've ever been so pleased to see anyone in my life." When Cat let go, she had tears in her eyes. Cupping Amelie's face with her hands, she rested her forehead on her sister's and whispered, "Please never stay away so long ever again. I've missed you."

Ignoring her second anxious twinge of the morning, Amelie whispered back, "I've missed you, too."

7
ROSE

W HILE N ONNA RETREATED to her kitchen to quickly rustle up some *real* pasta for Amelie's welcome home dinner, Rose pottered around the ranch house.

For years, upstairs had been firmly the domain of the family. But the downstairs areas were still divided into two main sections – shared rooms which the guests were allowed to use, and a few that were sealed off for the Goodwins only.

Nonna had her own living quarters out back that looked onto the kitchen garden and, while Rose and Thomas had always told her she was part of the family, she almost never intruded into what she considered to be *their* space.

Although the family spent most of their time in the kitchen, gathered around the large dining table, or outside, Rose swept and dusted the living room and set out a large vase of sunflowers on the coffee table. The room next door, which they always referred to as the 'library' because it was covered wall-to-wall with books that she and Thomas had collected over the years, was dusted too. And she placed two fresh baskets of lavender on the windowsill to take away the musty smell that inevitably accompanied so many old leather-bound volumes of text.

She was taking a moment to appreciate how lovely everywhere looked when the sound of knuckles knocking loudly on wood broke her concentration.

"Rose?" The door swung open and Jean – one of her most experienced members of staff – gingerly stuck his head into the room. "I'm so sorry to disturb you…"

"What is it?" Rose glanced down at her pocketless dress, realising that her phone was upstairs and not – as it usually was – on her person.

Jean grimaced. "It's Andante. We can't get her back into the stable."

Rose felt her jaw twitch. Her skin tightened. "Okay," she said. "I'm coming."

In the paddock furthest away from the stables, Andante – the wild black horse who had tossed Thomas from her back and caused so very many problems – was in a fury. Her eyes were wild, sweat glistened on her shoulders, and every time Jean tried to persuade her closer, she bolted.

"Normally, I'd let her stay out here, but we need the paddock for a group lesson," he said as Rose strode towards him.

Wishing she wasn't still wearing her red dress, Rose glanced up at the increasingly hot sun.

"Do you think she's sick? Or just in one of her tempers?"

"Whether she's sick or not," Jean said, "we need to calm her down or no one will be able to get close enough to take a look."

Rose looked back at the fence where three of their summer volunteers were waiting to pitch in. "Can someone fetch Dot, please?"

No one moved. "Now!"

Beside her, Jean laughed dolefully. "You really think that'll work?"

"It's worth a shot."

Kicking off her sandals, Rose ran barefoot to the fence and waved her hands at Felicia – one of the youngest volunteers. "I need your boots," she said, looking back at Jean, who had once again failed to talk Andante into slowing down as she cantered past.

"My boots?"

Beside Felicia, an English boy with an upper-class lilt to his voice said, "If the horse tramples on her in sandals, it'll break her feet." He widened his eyes. "So, hurry up?"

"Oh, of course." Cheeks flushing, Felicia bent down and unzipped her far-too-clean riding boots, then handed them over. They were too small, but Rose forced her feet in anyway.

"Right." She rubbed her hands together. "Let's see if this works."

A few moments later, the stable hand who'd heeded Rose's instruction returned. His cheeks were red, and he looked considerably out of puff, but behind him, ambling along as if he had all the time in the world, was Dot the donkey.

"Thank you," Rose said, taking hold of Dot's bridle and leading him into the paddock.

"What now?" Jean folded his arms in front of his chest.

"Now," said Rose, slipping Dot's bridle off his nose and giving him a kiss on the forehead, "we give these two some alone time."

Jean looked like he was about to protest, but bit his tongue and followed Rose out of the paddock.

"Come on," she said, beckoning for the others to follow. "We'll wait under the trees."

At first, nothing changed. Dot simply stood by the gate, his ears occasionally twitching away flies as he nibbled on a patch of grass. At the far end of the paddock, Andante whinnied and started off on another loop of the field.

But as she passed Dot, she slowed down a little.

Rose glanced at Jean, holding her breath. But he was watching too intently to notice.

After another loop, which didn't even cause Dot to raise his head, Andante stopped and puffed loudly through her nostrils. Dot looked up then, using the only speed he possessed – super slow – he meandered towards her.

Andante watched as the small grey donkey approached. When he was just a few feet in front of her, she scraped her left hoof on the ground and shook her mane. But then, just like that, she seemed to settle. Dot stopped beside her and stood – still as a statue – blinking at his friend.

Then, finally, Andante leaned towards him and touched

her nose to his side. Dot moved closer. And the pair of them were calm.

"That's amazing," breathed Felicia. "How did you know to do that?"

Rose looked at Felicia, who had no idea that the ranch used to be so much more than just her. "When Andante first came here, no one could get near her. It was my husband's idea to introduce her to Dot before we tried people," she said tightly. Then she patted Jean's arm and smiled. "Looks like Andante just needed a friend."

8

AMELIE

As they pulled up at the front of the ranch house, Cat and Ben's voices faded into the background and Amelie's heart fluttered. It had been eight months since she was last in Italy, but it felt like forever. When she first moved to London, she had visited every other month. Sometimes every six weeks. Often, she'd fly out to Tuscany on a Friday afternoon, spend Saturday and Sunday with her family, and get an early flight back to London in time for her Monday morning meeting.

After her father's accident, she should have visited more often. But it was around the same time that she had secured her promotion, and she had been so caught up in the excitement of it, and then in the engagement, and their potential house hunt…

Amelie laced her fingers together in her lap. "I stayed away too long," she breathed. But before she'd even finished, Cat's hand was on her shoulder.

"Stop being so melancholy. You're here to get married!

You should be buzzing with…" Cat waved her arms, "giddy, bridezilla excitement. Not all droopy and nostalgic."

Throwing open the truck door, her sister shouted, "Let's find Mum. I'm surprised she's not out here with a welcome party."

Amelie followed Cat and Ben up to the house. Guests were dotted here and there, down by the pool, and on the veranda drinking iced tea. In the distance, she could see that five horses and their riders, who had presumably been on a trek in the hills beyond the ranch, were arriving back at the stables. But there was no sign of her mother.

"Wait here," Ben said, leaving Amelie and Cat by the reception desk as if they were trying to check in for a long weekend break. "I'll go find her."

He was gone only seconds, but instead of returning with their mother he brought back Amelie's second-favourite maternal figure…

"Nonna!" Amelie squeaked and dashed forward to wrap her arms around the plump old woman who was already crying but pretending not to be.

"My baby," Nonna said, patting Amelie's hair. "You've come home to get married…" She stepped back and examined Amelie, eyeing her from head to toe. Then she scowled. "You've lost weight. Are you eating properly?"

Amelie laughed and patted her stomach, which admittedly was a little flatter than it had been a few months ago; Jed had insisted that the two of them try a 'clean eating' pre-wedding diet in order to shift a few pounds before the big day. But Amelie didn't dare mention the word 'diet' in Nonna's presence, so she just glanced towards the kitchen and said, "I'm sure you've got some treats back there that could fatten me up."

Nonna grinned and took her hands away from her hips. "Sit down. The three of you. I will bring food and drinks while you wait for your mother."

As Nonna disappeared, and the siblings headed back outside, Amelie nudged Ben. "Wait for Mum? Where is she?"

"A problem with one of the horses, apparently," Ben replied, his lips tighter than normal.

"What is it?" Amelie ducked to meet his eyes.

Ben inhaled slowly, his nostrils flaring the same way that Ethan's did. Cat had stopped too, and both women were watching him expectantly. Finally, Ben said, "She's been pretty stressed. It hasn't been easy since Dad left."

Amelie swallowed hard. She hated to think of her mother struggling, and the wedding invitation addressed to her father that she'd been carrying around with her suddenly felt like a guilty secret weighing her down – as if she shouldn't *want* him to be there because of everything he'd put them through.

"Is it really that bad?" Cat had folded her arms in front of her chest and was raising her customary eyebrow. Clearly, despite the fact she lived nearby, this was the first she was hearing of it too.

Ben opened his mouth to speak, but then shook his head at them. "Don't say anything. She's trying to put a brave face on for Amelie and the wedding. She wouldn't want me to–"

Amelie squeezed Ben's forearm. "We get it." But before she could delve deeper into what her brother meant by 'not easy', Nonna reappeared with a huge tray of food, which she set down on a large round table on the veranda.

"Come," she called. "Sit and tell Nonna what you've been up to. All of you. It has been too long since I saw your smiling faces beside one another."

Beside Amelie, Ben leaned down and whispered, "You and Cat catch up with Nonna, I'll go see if Mum needs any help."

"I could–"

"It's fine, Am. You've had a long morning. Relax, get settled in. I'll see you in a bit."

Cat was already sitting down, one long tanned leg crossed over the other, pouring herself a glass of tea. But Amelie lingered, watching Ben stride off down the track that led to the stables. Something wasn't quite right. Something she couldn't name, or clasp hold of, that was floating under the surface of her brother's words and her mother's absence, making her skin feel tight and prickly.

As Ben's silhouette faded into the distance, Amelie turned back to her sister and shook her arms to release the feeling. Spread out on Nonna's tray was a selection of thick-cut meats, gloriously rich cheeses, and coffee with cream. Watching Cat bite into a huge chunk of bread, loaded with cheese and salami, a smile came to Amelie's lips and she flopped down in the chair beside Nonna. *There goes the diet,* she thought as she reached for the cheese.

For over an hour, Amelie and Cat drank in the luscious tones of Nonna's voice as she regaled them with stories from her kitchen. As it turned out, she had a new assistant *and* a new chicken. Neither of which was working out particularly well.

As she stood, and gathered the empty tray and the coffee pot, Nonna shrugged. "What can I say? She's young and inexperienced, so she was very cheap."

"The hen or the cook?" Cat was already laughing, and when she caught Amelie's eye the feeling was contagious.

"Both!" Nonna boomed, tipping her head back. "Both!" When she'd finished guffawing at the sky, she wiped her watery eyes with the back of her hand. "I'll fetch more coffee. Your mother will be back soon, I'm sure."

Amelie glanced at Cat; she wasn't sure she could handle more caffeine and – with Nonna – coffee *never* came alone. It would be accompanied by something delicious that she wouldn't be able to resist, and she was already noticing the tug of her waistband and wishing she'd changed into a floaty dress on arrival.

"Sounds wonderful." Cat lazed back in her chair and pulled her sunglasses down to cover her eyes. Resting her hands behind her head, she sighed. "I really should come up here more often. I get so sucked into work and…" she trailed off, but Amelie knew what she was about to say.

"And *Mister Gelato*?"

She couldn't see her sister's eyes but knew that Cat would have narrowed them at her as she replied, "His name is Filippo."

"And will *Filippo* be coming to the wedding?" Amelie made a show of getting a notebook out of her purse and flipping to the page containing the guest list. "I just want to make sure he's not left out…"

"He'll probably be busy with the store. But I'll ask."

Amelie closed the notebook and bit her lower lip. She wanted to highlight the fact that, surely, Cat should have asked him already – seeing as the wedding was only a few weeks away. But she didn't. With Cat, it was always far too easy to slide from being best friends to sworn enemies. In fact, similar to the twins, Amelie recalled them spending most of their childhood either in one another's pockets or stomping around declaring that they would no longer be speaking. Ever.

So, she bit her tongue and instead gazed out at the landscape that she knew better than anywhere else in the world.

She was watching a family group of two older women – who looked like either best friends or sisters – and three teenage children splash around in the pool when Cat nudged her. "Mum's back," she grinned.

Instantly, Amelie sprung up from her chair. Unable to contain her excitement, and despite the sun that was bearing down on the veranda, she jogged towards her mother, waving and smiling as if they had been apart for far longer than eight months.

"Mum!"

Stopping a few feet in front of her mother, Amelie put her hands on her hips, looked Mum up and down, and laughed.

"I know," her mother replied. "I must look an absolute mess." She wafted an unruly wisp of hair from her face and looked down at her legs, which sported a pair of knee-high riding boots that stood out in complete contrast to the smart red tea dress on her upper half. Smoothing her dress with her palms, she shrugged. "You know what it's like around here."

"I do," Amelie stepped forward and wrapped her arms around her mum's neck, snuggling into her and breathing in the familiar scent of her perfume mixed with hay and horses. "I do know what it's like. And I can't tell you how good it is to be back."

9

ROSE

As soon as Rose saw her youngest daughter, her heart lifted. Pulling Amelie close, she saw Cat in the distance and smiled. In capri pants and a striped boat neck t-shirt, Cat looked as decadent as ever. She was reclining in one of the chairs on the veranda and waved casually from behind an enormous pair of sunglasses when she spotted her mother looking in her direction.

Rose waved back, then looped her arm through Amelie's. "You must be sweltering," she said as they walked towards Catherine.

Amelie glanced down at her jeans and flapped a hand at her face, which was a little flushed. "I am. But I wanted to wait for you before going upstairs."

"Well," Rose said, nudging closer, "why don't we both go freshen up and then we can catch up properly?"

"Sounds good." Amelie gave a little sigh as she leaned into Rose's shoulder.

On the veranda, Rose kissed Cat's cheek and playfully tapped one of her large red earrings with her index finger. "Love the earrings, darling," she said, knowing it would make Cat smile. "They go perfectly with that shade of lipstick."

"Thanks, Mum," Cat replied, grinning in the same way she had as a teenager whenever Rose had helped her curl her hair or apply mascara.

Then, turning to Amelie, Rose said, "Amelie, sweetheart, about your accommodation... I have a bit of a surprise. I've reserved you the best cabin. I know I said it was already booked, but it was a little white lie." She smiled as Amelie's eyes widened. "It's ready now, but it's totally up to you whether you stay in the house until Jed arrives or..."

Amelie grinned and jigged up and down. "Mum, that's amazing." She bit her lower lip thoughtfully and looked towards the cabins. The honeymoon cabin was positioned in a little nook all of its own, with stunning views over the ranch and the surrounding hills. But then Amelie turned away and stared up at the ranch house. The big sash window at the front of the house belonged to her bedroom, and it had been hers ever since she arrived on Rose and Thomas's doorstep as a shy, petite, little girl with pigtails and dimpled cheeks. "Jed will love the cabin, but I think I'd like to stay in the house with you guys for a while."

"Well then, that's perfect." Rose felt the tension drop from her shoulders, unexpectedly thrilled that Amelie had picked the main house. "Your room's all ready, just like always, and there are fresh towels in the family bathroom."

"Great. My bags are in the truck. Mind if I go get changed?"

Rose nodded and waved her hand at the front of the house. "Of course not. I'll see you in a while." She turned to Cat and was about to tell her that she, too, needed to shower. But Cat spoke before she had the chance to.

Looking at her phone, Cat was grimacing. "Mum, can I use your computer for a while? It's great to see Am and everything, but I wasn't expecting to come up here until this evening and I need to..."

Although she wasn't entirely sure what gelato-related computer work Cat could possibly have to do so urgently, Rose nodded. "Sure. If we go through reception, I'll give you the key to the office. You can use it as long as you like."

"Fabulous."

Cat followed Rose through the house, then swiftly set herself up in the room that had begun – so many years ago – as Rose's workplace. "Thanks, Mum," she said nonchalantly, offering a slight wave but not really paying attention to where her mother was.

"You're welcome. See you soon."

As she watched Cat sit down behind the computer and give her bouncy shoulder-length hair a little flick, Rose smiled to herself. Even now, every time she looked out through the window in front of the desk which framed the ranch and the hills beyond, she was reminded of just how magical *Heart of the Hills* had always been to her.

Thirty years later, the way she felt when she decided to make the ranch her home still tingled on her skin. Leaving England to marry a handsome ranch owner had seemed so adventurous, so daring, and so incredibly romantic. Thomas had promised her the world and, for far longer than she ever thought possible, he had given it to her.

After everything, she should probably try to simply remember the good times, to count herself lucky for having so many years of happiness, and to move on. Leave the past behind. Start fresh.

But when every fibre of the ranch held whispers of Thomas, how could she?

When her entire life was entwined with his, how could she possibly live a life that didn't include him?

Upstairs, in her hollow, creaky bedroom, Rose closed the door and leaned against it. She could hear Amelie singing in the shower – loud and out of tune. Cat was home. Ben was helping Jean with Andante, but would soon be back up at the house, ready to tuck into a hearty meal. And in a fortnight, Ethan would be there too. All four of her children would be under the same roof – laughing, bickering, and driving her mad.

She couldn't wait. And as she padded through to her en suite and made a mental note to return Felicia's boots, her heart filled with a sense of tranquillity. Soon, her family would be back together. There would be dinners, and long walks, treks in the hills, splashing in the pool. And a wedding at the end of it.

But as quickly as the calmness washed over her, it was replaced with a swirling cloud of trepidation. The siblings hadn't been together – all four of them – since before Thomas left. And Rose really wasn't sure how they would handle his absence, especially when she broke the news that she was thinking of selling their home.

A few hours later, Rose placed a huge bowl of steaming pasta in the centre of the dining table. Amelie, who'd been helping her cook, grabbed a bottle of red wine from the countertop and poured them a small glass each.

"Smells delicious, Mum," she said, licking her lower lip and swirling the wine around the bottom of her glass. "But how can I still be starving hungry after all the snacks Nonna tempted me with?"

Rose put her arm around Amelie's waist and pulled her close for a hug. "Because you've clearly been dieting, and your poor little stomach is thrilled that it's being presented with *proper* food."

Amelie tutted and rolled her eyes but didn't protest too much. And, as if by magic, Cat and Ben appeared from outside.

"Smells gorgeous," Cat said, echoing her sister as Ben pushed the large glass doors so they were wide open and letting in a gentle breeze.

Rose waved at the table. "Sit, all of you, sit." Then she reached for her iPad. "Shall I see if I can get Ethan? I'm sure he's horribly jealous at the thought of missing out on being with you all." As she spoke, she watched Ben. She knew that the two of them weren't really speaking, and it was something she was desperate to fix.

It wouldn't take much; as soon as they were together, they'd forget that they were in a fight. But, for now, Ben continued to resist the idea.

"He'll be at work, Mum," he said, sliding into a seat beside Cat and starting to pile food onto his plate.

"Okay." She put the iPad back down and took the chair next to Amelie. "We'll try later, then."

Ben nodded curtly, and Rose caught the girls exchanging a glance that said, *Huh. So, the twins still aren't speaking.* Changing the subject, she looked at Ben. "How was Andante when you left her?"

"Better," he said, brightening. "Good. The trick with Dot was good thinking."

Amelie and Cat were watching the two of them, so Rose explained what had happened. Taking a sip of wine, she added, "I'm glad it worked."

"Are you going to keep her?" Cat's eyebrow was raised, in her trademark style.

Rose put her glass down and pinched its stem with her thumb and index finger. Looking at each child in turn, she said, "I don't know. Your father wanted to. But..."

"He's not here," Cat finished bluntly.

Rose swallowed hard. Ben was silent. And then Amelie said, "Has *anyone* heard from him? I mean, do we even know if he's okay?"

Rose bit back a sigh; she'd hoped to avoid this discussion until at least a few hours into the evening. But she tried not to let her feelings show on her face as she replied lightly, "He's in touch with Aunt Katie. But, no, I haven't heard from him. As far as I know, he's fine."

Amelie was looking down at her plate, moving her food around with her fork as if she'd suddenly lost her appetite. "I was just thinking about the wedding, and..."

Rose's stomach lurched uncomfortably. A claw of anger scratched sharply at her belly whenever she thought of the fact that Thomas hadn't even told Amelie whether he'd be walking her down the aisle on her wedding day. "Do you have an invitation for him? If we give it to Katie, I'm sure she'll pass it on."

Opposite her sister, Cat opened her mouth as if she was about to speak, but Rose looked at her pointedly – now was not the time. Miraculously, Cat took the hint.

"Okay." Amelie nodded. "I understand if he doesn't feel like he can come. I just need to know."

Rose patted Amelie's leg beneath the table. "Of course you do."

"Well, if he doesn't," Ben said, clearly trying to lighten the mood, "you could always ask Skye to fill his place, so the food doesn't go to waste."

"Skye?" Rose put her fork down with a loud clatter. "Anderson?"

"Mmm." Amelie was chewing and waving her hand as she tried to hurry up so that she could speak. "I forgot to tell you. I bumped into him on the plane. He and Alec are staying in *Sant Anna* for a few weeks."

"Really?" Rose was certain that her cheeks were turning pink. She felt hot and cold at the same time, and her skin was prickling. Alec had told her that Skye would be joining him on his visit, but he'd promised that the two of them would stay out of the way of the ranch until Rose had told the children what was happening. "How is he? Was Alec with him?" she asked, piling more salad onto her plate even though it was already full.

"Good. He seemed good." Amelie put down her fork and waved her hand as she told the others that Alec was already in the area, and that Skye was meeting his dad for a vacation. "He didn't say much about it, but I think he only recently left the Army. Seems like he needs a bit of a rest."

"Odd that they'd come to *Sant Anna* but not to the ranch," Cat said. "And a bit of a shame. I wouldn't say no to watching Skye Anderson strut around the place for a few days. Especially if he's now army-level attractive."

Ignoring her sister's comment but looking a little flustered, Amelie said, "Well, they stayed at the ranch pretty much every year for a decade. They probably wanted a change of scenery."

"Or it was too much. You know..." Ben said solemnly, dampening the girls' giddiness, "with remembering his Mum and everything."

As a delicate quiet settled on the table, Rose placed her palms firmly down on its top and attempted to steer the conversation away from the Andersons. "So, Amelie. The wedding... tell us everything. What's left to plan? Have you settled on the food? And–"

"And when do we get to see the dress?" Cat cut in, her eyes wide and excited.

Amelie's lips spread into a grin. "Oh, Cat," she said. "I can't *wait* for you to see it."

As the girls chatted about dresses, accessories, and shoes, Ben groaned loudly. "And here we go..." He rolled his eyes but grinned cheekily. "Let the torture begin."

Relaxing a little, but not completely, Rose fixed her eyes on her children and tried to concentrate on what they were saying. But, somehow, the fact that Amelie had come into contact with Skye made everything feel real. Too real.

If Alec agreed to buy the ranch, Rose would have to tell the children that their home would no longer be their home. And that their father was the cause of it.

Nearly two hours later, having exhausted wedding talk and consumed more food than she'd thought possible, Rose stood up and began to gather the plates. She took Cat and Ben's first, then held out her hand and gestured for Amelie to pass over her dish. But Amelie was absorbed in her phone. Rose wiggled her fingers at her daughter. "Any time now, Am..." she nudged gently.

When Amelie didn't reply, Cat waved a hand in front of her sister's face. "Amelie. Dish."

"Oh..." Amelie looked up, dazedly handed her plate to her mother, then gestured to her phone. "Mum, Skye just texted me. He's asking if we have any spare cabins. The Airbnb they booked has fallen through – the guy just didn't show up and the neighbours say they haven't seen him for weeks."

Rose felt her features stiffen. The thought of Alec staying

at the ranch made her feel skin feel clammy. But she already knew what Amelie was going to say.

Shrugging, as if the answer was simple, Amelie began to text. "I'll just tell them to take the honeymoon cabin." She glanced up at Rose. "That's okay, right? No one's using it, and they can move out before Jed arrives."

Opposite Amelie, Cat was smiling. "Can't say I'm unhappy about the idea of Skye being on site for a few weeks. Maybe he can make a guest appearance at the hen-do?"

Amelie rolled her eyes at her sister. "I'm not having a hen-do. I already told you that." Then she looked at Rose. "Mum?"

Rose gripped the edge of the table but tried to keep smiling. "Of course, sweetheart. No problem. Tell Skye that he and Alec are welcome to come stay."

10

AMELIE

AT RIDICULOUS-O'CLOCK THE NEXT MORNING, Nonna's cockerel crowed and Amelie prised her eyes open. It was already bright outside; the thin cream curtains fluttering as an uncustomary breeze drifted in through the open windows.

As Amelie reached instinctively for her phone to check her inbox for emails from work, she stopped herself. Of course, there would be none; she had no job. No authors to worry about. No manuscripts to read. She'd offered to keep an eye on things for a few weeks, but HR had already arranged for anything addressed to her to be forwarded on to her replacement.

Holding the phone in her hand, she tapped her fingernails on the screen. She knew Jed wouldn't have tried to contact her; he was hopeless at keeping in touch when she wasn't in the immediate vicinity. So, for the first time in far too many years, instead of checking for text messages or beginning the day with a dose of pessimism from a daily news site, she put the device down on her bedside table and let her head snuggle back into her pillow.

For another hour, she dozed, mulling over things that needed to be done to prepare for the wedding, and thinking of how lovely it had been to be with Ben, and Catherine, and her mother the night before. Briefly, she thought of her father. But, as had become customary, she pushed the thought away.

She'd be seeing her aunt Katie in a few days for wedding dress shopping and, like her mum suggested, she would give the wedding invitation to Katie when they saw one another. And that would be that. He'd either come or not come; there was nothing she could do about it.

Yawning and sitting up, she looked towards the window. Skye and his father would be waking up in the best cabin the ranch had to offer. But Amelie didn't mind. Seeing the Andersons arrive last night, even though it was horribly late and her mother looked strangely stressed by the last-minute intrusion, had been soothingly nostalgic.

When they were kids, she and Cat, and the twins, would hang around impatiently for hours at the start of the summer, waiting for Skye and his parents to arrive. As soon as he stepped out of the car, they'd all bolt down to the pool and spend the next few weeks with Skye as an extra member of the pack.

Those summers were still some of the fondest memories she had – so different from the way life had started out for both her and her sister.

Eventually, Amelie stopped daydreaming and forced herself out of bed. Tugging a pale blue dressing gown from her suitcase, she wrapped it around herself and headed downstairs.

Cat had returned home late last night, taking the taxi that had brought Skye and Alec up to the ranch, and Ben and her mother would already be down with the horses. So, the kitchen was eerily quiet.

Amelie sighed contentedly and pushed open the doors, allowing the cool morning air to drift in. Out back, Nonna's hens were strutting through the kitchen gardens, pecking at the ground in a way that had always made her chuckle.

Enjoying the solitude, she made some coffee, piled yogurt onto a bowl full of fruit, and sat for a while thinking of precisely nothing.

Next door, she could hear guests in the main dining room, gobbling up Nonna's lavish breakfast and preparing themselves for a day of trekking, lessons, or relaxing by the pool.

Amelie glanced at her watch – it was nearly nine. She should address one of the many items on her to-do list, but she felt oddly lethargic; all she really wanted to do was soak up the feeling of being home.

By the time she'd consumed another coffee – decaf this time – and washed up her dishes, it was closer to ten and there was still no sign of her mother or Ben. So, she dashed upstairs, pulled on some shorts and a loose-fitting t-shirt, and headed down towards the stables to look for them.

She was part-way there, ducking down onto the path that led behind the swimming pool, when she heard Skye call her name. She turned, and he jogged to catch up with her.

"Hey." He wasn't even a little out of breath. "Long time, no see."

"I hope you slept okay," she said, although it would be pretty much impossible not to sleep well in the honeymoon cabin.

"Are you kidding? Best sleep ever." Skye grinned, then nodded at the path ahead. "Where are you headed?"

"I thought I'd see if I can find Mum or Ben. Failing that, I'll probably try to blag a horse from Jean and go for a ride." She put her hands into her pockets. "You?"

"Dad's still sleeping – jet lag – so I was going to walk off some of Nonna's breakfast. Or maybe swim."

"I'm sure I can blag *two* horses, if you're up for it?"

Skye followed her as she started walking. "Sure. But it's been years since I rode a horse."

"You didn't ride in the Army?"

As Amelie looked at him, Skye pressed his lips together before saying, "No, I was with a canine unit."

Amelie was about to ask more questions, because she still hadn't formed a very complete picture of what Skye did in the Veterinary Corps, but something about his demeanour told her not to. "Well," she said casually. "I don't do it too regularly either, these days. But you don't forget how, and you spent enough summers out here as a kid for it to be second nature."

"Where shall we ride to?" Skye asked, looking towards the hills beyond the ranch.

"The creek?"

Skye's lips tightened and moved to the side in a slightly pained expression. "I love the creek but the route's not easy, is it?"

Surprised at his reluctance, Amelie put her hand on

Skye's upper arm and said, "Don't worry. I'll look after you. Besides, the horses know the way by heart. We'll be in safe hands."

"Don't you mean safe *hooves*?"

Amelie laughed unexpectedly loudly. "Wow. That was a dad-level joke if ever I heard one."

Skye was shaking his head and had put his hand across his eyes. "I know. I knew it was bad even as I was saying it." He parted his fingers just enough so he could look out between them. "I told you I got awkward since we were kids."

"See," Amelie said as they reached the bottom of a sharp rocky slope which had caused them to dismount and walk beside the horses. "I told you it'd be fine."

Skye was standing next to his horse, Shadow, and stroking her flank. "You did a good job," he said to her softly. "A real good job." Looking at Amelie, he smiled a lop-sided smile and shook his head. "That was tough."

"But fun?"

"Oh, for sure," he said, climbing back into Shadow's saddle and taking hold of the reins once more.

"Well, this bit's even *more* fun." Amelie's horse Rupert was slowly munching some blackberries he'd found on a nearby bush but when she tapped his sides firmly with her heels, he began to trot. As the trot turned to a canter, and the canter turned into a full-blown gallop, Amelie shouted, "Last one to the creek is a loser!"

With the wind whipping through her hair and across her face, she tore across the meadow on Rupert's back. Soon, Skye was beside her and when she looked at him, he was smiling.

Reaching the forest on the other side, the horses instinctively slowed down and trotted beneath the shade of the canopy. The creek wasn't far from the edge of the trees and, as if they knew exactly where Skye and Amelie had planned to go, Shadow and Rupert wound their way there with little direction from their riders.

Dismounting at the water's edge, Amelie gave Rupert and Shadow a carrot each and sat down on a nearby rock. Letting out a short, contented *ahh*, Skye sat down beside her.

"That was good," he said. "Really good."

"Best feeling in the world," Amelie agreed.

Looking back at the horses and then at the backpack she'd brought with her, Skye raised his eyebrows. "D'you bring us snacks too? Or just those guys?"

"You ate one of Nonna's breakfasts and you're still hungry?"

"I'm always hungry," Skye said.

"I guess you army dudes need a lot of feeding." Amelie smiled as she took another carrot from her bag and tossed it to him. "There, that'll have to do for now."

Skye looked crestfallen. Flexing his arm muscles ironically at her, he waved the carrot and said, "You don't get muscles like these from eating carrots. Come on, Goodwin. What else have you got in there?"

In response, Amelie made an exaggerated show of rummaging around in her bag. When she looked up, she widened her eyes. "Oh," she said, "look what I found." Tossing a chocolate bar at him, she took one for herself too and, after taking a huge bite of it, leaned back on her hands. "You know," she said, mouth still half full of chocolate, "I'm supposed to be dieting."

"What the heck for?" Skye crumpled his chocolate wrapper into a ball and shoved it into his jeans pocket.

"Um. The wedding?" Amelie was twirling the remaining three-quarters of her bar around her fingers and looking at it longingly. "I really shouldn't eat this."

"Well, I'll give you approximately ten seconds to decide. And then I'm having it." Skye moved to snatch it from her, but Amelie pulled it out of his reach.

"I said I *shouldn't* eat it, not that I *wouldn't*," she said, peeling off the rest of the packaging and giving in to temptation.

"You know." Skye kicked off his boots. "I've never understood why women go on wedding diets. You should look like *you* when you walk down the aisle. Not an under-nourished version of you."

Amelie had finished eating and was now, like Skye, preparing to dip her feet in the water. "Well…" she said, but then stopped. "Actually, you know what, let's not talk about the wedding. Let's just enjoy the peace and quiet up here for a while."

Skye had waded into the creek and was watching fast, shallow water bubble over his toes. "Sounds good to me," he said.

For a while, they stood beside one another without speaking. The sun was shining; the sky was a perfect powder blue, and all Amelie could hear was the babbling of the creek, birds in the trees, and the soft swaying of the branches as a breeze caught their leaves. When she looked at Skye, he had his eyes closed.

"You know," he said, smiling with the corner of his mouth in a way that made his cheek dimple beneath its stubble. "My mum loved it up here. Dad always preferred the routes towards the beach, but me and mom did this one a fair few times."

Although it was warm, Amelie wrapped her arms around herself as a small delicate shiver crept up her spine. "Skye," she said. "I meant to tell you on the plane how sorry I was about your mum; I just wasn't sure what to say."

Skye shook his head. "That's okay. I'm still not sure what to say about it either." Shrugging and putting his hands into his pockets, he added, "People ask how I'm doing, and I tell them I'm fine but…"

"How could you ever be *fine* about it?"

"Exactly."

"Well, if you ever want to talk about her…" Amelie smiled and hoped she was saying the right thing. "I'm happy to listen. I have such fond memories of all of us together."

Skye was tracing Amelie's features with his eyes, grazing over the freckles that splashed the bridge of her nose, and the flush on her cheeks from their gallop across the meadow. "Thank you," he said, clearing his throat as his voice wavered. Then he smiled. "You know," he said, "I was thinking today about the way she used to pick up on these 'cool' phrases the kids were using and try to use them herself." Laughing, he bent down, picked up a stone, and skimmed it across the surface of the water. "I would be so embarrassed over it, but I'm pretty sure that once she realised, she did it deliberately just to mess with me."

Amelie laughed. "That sounds like something my dad would do."

Skye weighed a small stone up and down in his hand. "And she told the worst jokes," he said. "Like, the *worst*. But her cooking was incredible."

As Skye fell into easy and happy remembering, Amelie smiled and let him talk. Somehow, the sound of his voice was almost as soothing as the sound of the creek itself. And by the time they climbed back onto their horses and started the return journey to the ranch, both she and Skye seemed lighter.

11
ROSE

JUST BEFORE MIDDAY, Rose finished in the stables and returned to the house. She was halfway up the steps out front when she heard Alec call her name.

Last night, she had purposefully avoided his and Skye's arrival; she was certain that the way she looked at Alec, or spoke to him, would expose the fact that they were hiding something from the kids. And she wasn't ready to have that conversation – not yet.

"Rose..." Alec repeated, jogging to catch up with her. "I'm so sorry about last night. We'll be out of your hair as soon as possible. I know it must be awkward for you."

"I haven't told the children–"

"I know." Alec smiled reassuringly at her and waved up at the house. "Do you have time for a chat?"

"Sure." Rose continued up the steps, through reception, and towards the family kitchen where she flicked on the coffee machine and poured herself a glass of water.

"You look beat," Alec said. "Why don't you sit? All I've been doing all morning is soaking up the incredible views from the cabin."

"We call it the honeymoon cabin." Rose sat down, crossing one leg over the other, and rubbing at her ankle. "Best on the ranch."

Alec turned and leaned back against the counter. And as he did, the sudden role-reversal caught Rose off guard; if she sold the ranch to Alec, if he made her an offer and she accepted it, this would become *his* kitchen. And if she ever returned to *Heart of the Hills*, it would be as a guest.

"Alec, I hate to ask but does Skye know the reason you're here?" She stopped rubbing her foot and folded her arms in front of her chest. "I mean, have you told him you're thinking of buying the ranch? Or does he think you're just out here on holiday?"

Behind him, the coffee machine beeped. Alec turned to it, pressed the button, and allowed a stream of hot coffee to spurt into the cup below. When he turned back to her, he nodded. "I told him last night. But he knows that it's confidential. He won't say anything to the others."

A trill of panic fluttered in Rose's chest. "Are you sure? Because he and Amelie have always been thick as thieves..." She tried to smile, but it didn't reach her lips.

"I'm sure," Alec said. "He knows it's a delicate situation."

Rose nodded, accepting the mug he handed her and taking a sip even though it was too hot. "And will Skye be helping you run the place?" She paused and tilted her head. "*If* you decide it's something you want."

Alec walked over slowly and sat down opposite her, resting his mug on the table and leaning forward on his elbows. "That's the idea, yes." He drummed his fingers on the table, then stopped and picked his mug back up. "He's had a tough couple of years. First, his mother. And then leaving the Army."

"Amelie mentioned that. I didn't know he'd joined."

Alec's expression was a lot more stoic than it was a moment ago. "He did. But now... well, he needs something different. A new challenge. A fresh start. We both do. Most of my businesses pretty much take care of themselves now and, to be honest, since Della passed away, my heart hasn't been in the consultancy work. Travelling all over the world to help guys in fancy suits make more money to buy more fancy suits doesn't feel too important anymore. You know?"

Rose smiled with one side of her mouth. "Well, I certainly understand that. I can't imagine how difficult it must have been for the two of you..." Then before she had really even thought about what she was saying, she added, "Listen, why don't you and Skye stay at *Heart of the Hills* for a while? It'd be a good opportunity for you to get to know the place a little better. And I think the kids are pleased to see Skye."

Alec hesitated. "Are you sure?"

"Yes. I'm sure." Rose leaned into the hard wooden back of her chair; these days, a morning's work in the stables left her considerably achier than it used to. "Selling is the right thing to do. I'm serious about it, Alec. But I don't want you to do me any favours. You need to be sure it's the right thing for you and Skye."

Alec inclined his head, slipping quickly into a more business-like tone of voice. "Okay. Sure. We'll stay. I'll shadow you while you work, spend some time looking over all the details, and then we can talk again about our options. How does that sound?"

Rose had been holding her breath and released it slowly. "It sounds like a plan."

"Great. So, what's next?" Alec rubbed his hands together as if he was ready to get to work.

"Next?" Rose smiled. "Next, we eat lunch."

At one o'clock, just as the guests were starting to appear in the dining hall for lunch, Skye and Amelie arrived back from their trek. Sun-kissed and smiling, they entered the kitchen and flopped down at the table.

Rose looked at Alec and knew he was thinking the same as her – that their children were all grown up but that, somehow, they looked the same as they had when they were teenagers. The way Amelie's hair tumbled messily over her shoulders. The way Skye started picking at the dish of olives in front of him, causing Amelie to tap the top of his hand and say, "Oi."

Rose set a large jug of water down in the middle of the table. "It's okay, you guys can start. You look famished."

"I forgot how tough it is, riding up and down the hills near the creek." Skye was piling salad leaves onto his plate and topping them with olives, fresh tomatoes, and onions.

"You went up to the creek?" Rose sat down beside

Amelie, surprised that her daughter had attempted one of the more difficult routes after not having ridden for so many months.

Amelie, who already had a mouthful of bread, nodded. "Mmm. It's so peaceful up there. After London, I needed… peaceful."

"You don't like London?" Next to Rose, Alec looked up from his plate, clearly interested in Amelie's answer.

"I do," she said hesitantly. "But it's so busy. Hectic. Everyone's got somewhere to be and something to do. No one ever stops. *I* never stopped."

"Well…" Rose poured them each a glass of water. "That's because your work is so full on. How did they react to you taking so much time off for the wedding? Were they okay with it?"

Amelie nodded quickly. Something flickered in her face, but it was gone before Rose could figure out what it was. "They were fine with it." Changing the subject, she asked, "Where's Ben? Doesn't he come up to the house for lunch?"

"He's out trekking today." Rose looked at the clock. "He'll be back just before sundown."

"I didn't realise Ben led the treks." Amelie's forehead crinkled as though she was trying to work out why she hadn't known this about her brother.

"He's pretty good at it, actually." Rose took out her phone, scrolled to some pictures of Ben with the guests, and showed the screen to Amelie. "The guests really seem to like him."

"Well, that's good." Amelie glanced at Skye, then added, "When Ben quit medical school, we weren't really sure what he was going to do." Then she looked at Rose. "But if he enjoys working here and he's good at it, then maybe you and Dad will get your wish after all..."

Rose smiled nervously. "Our wish?"

"For a Goodwin kid to grow up and take over the ranch." Amelie smiled light-heartedly and rolled her eyes. And when Rose didn't respond, she teased, "Oh, come on, don't pretend you haven't always been a little disappointed that none of us wanted to run the business."

Rose forced out a laugh, deliberately avoiding Alec's gaze. Then, thankfully, Skye stepped in and changed the subject by asking about the wedding. As Amelie listed the many things that she hadn't yet finalised, Rose got up and walked over to the sink to refill the water jug. Catching her reflection in the mirrored tiles behind the taps, she sighed.

She and Thomas had always dreamed of one of the children taking over *Heart of the Hills*. They had talked about it staying in the family for generations, about spending time there with their grandchildren, enjoying long lazy summers and picturesque winters once they eventually retired and handed the daily running of the place over to the kids.

They had, however, quickly dismissed the idea as the children grew older; Ethan and Ben wanted to become doctors. Amelie wanted to be a writer. And Cat didn't know what she wanted to be.

How ironic that now it wasn't a possibility, Ben seemed to be changing his mind. How ironic that now she was being forced to say goodbye when the future they'd always imagined for the place was lingering just out of reach.

12

AMELIE

AFTER NEARLY A WEEK back at *Heart of the Hills*, Amelie was beginning to feel as if she'd never left. Each morning, she woke to glorious sunshine and the sound of Nonna's cockerel. Then she ate breakfast with her mum and Ben, followed them down to the stables, and helped with the horses. Around ten thirty, Skye would appear and the two of them would head off for a ride, spending most of the day out in the woods and hills surrounding the ranch before returning in time for Amelie to squeeze in a few wedding-related tasks before dinner.

"You've gone riding with Skye every day since you got here?"

It was eight thirty on the sixth day of Amelie's visit, and Cat had driven up to the ranch to join them for breakfast.

"Yes," Amelie replied noncommittally while piling some fruit and yogurt into a bowl.

Cat glanced at Ben, and Amelie noticed them exchange a 'look'.

"We're friends," she said, rolling her eyes. "Please tell me we're past the age where boys and girls can't possibly just be friends?"

Clearing his throat, Ben concentrated on buttering some toast, but Cat couldn't help herself. With a glint of mischief in her eyes, she nudged Amelie with her elbow and said, "Maybe. If the boy in question didn't look like Skye Anderson."

As their mother sat down and poured tea from a pot in the centre of the table, Amelie looked at her and said, in a slightly whiny voice, "Mum, tell her?"

"I'm with Ben," Mum said, smiling. "I'm not getting involved... although Skye *is* rather handsome."

All four of them were laughing, and Amelie was about to change the subject by asking her sister how Mr. Gelato was doing, when her phone rang. Looking down at it, she rose quickly from the table "It's Jed," she said, brushing her hand across her lips as if he would know just from the sound of her voice that she was no longer following their diet plan.

Stepping away from the table and out into the garden, Amelie lifted the phone to her ear. "Hey, stranger."

"Amelie..." Jed's voice was loud and sleepy. He yawned. "I set an alarm so I could call you before work. How are you?"

"Good, I'm good. How's London? How's the apartment? I've texted a few times, but..."

"Sorry, babe." There was that nickname again. "Work has been murder. So busy. Should be easing off soon though."

Amelie scraped her foot on the ground, listening to the stones crunch beneath it. "Ah, so I guess you haven't had time to–"

"House hunt?" Jed laughed loudly. "Not a chance, I'm afraid, Am. It can wait until you're back though, can't it? You're better at that kind of thing, anyway." Jed stifled another yawn, then chortled, "Besides, you'll have plenty of time, won't you? Now that you're a kept woman."

Amelie felt her forehead crease. "A *kept* woman?"

Still chuckling at himself, Jed seemed not to notice the tone of her voice, and simply replied, "Okay, Am. I have to go. I just wanted to say hi and that I love you. And good luck with the dress shopping today."

"You remembered?"

"Of course. Love you. Bye."

Back inside, her siblings and her mother looked up from their breakfast to stare at her expectantly.

"It was Jed," she offered, sitting back down and smiling thinly. "He was calling to wish me luck with the dress shopping."

"You'll need it." Cat sat back and sipped her coffee. "I can't believe you haven't actually seen the dress in person. What if you hate it? What if you change your mind? There won't be time to get another one."

Amelie heard her mother tut at Cat's directness, but simply rolled her eyes. "Of course, I won't hate it. I saw it in a magazine months before Jed and I even got engaged. I cut it out and kept it in my purse. It's…" Amelie released a sigh and hugged her arms around her middle. "It's stunning. You'll see."

Three hours later, Amelie, Cat, and their mother stepped into a boutique wedding dress shop in *Sant Anna* and shook hands with Sofia, the smiling shop owner. With long black hair, she looked typically Italian and had a bright white smile that was too perfect to be natural.

"Good morning, Goodwin family," she said smoothly, first in English and then Italian.

"Hi, Sofia, I'm Amelie. It's so lovely to meet in person." Amelie and Sofia had spoken many times on the phone, but this was the first time they'd been in the same room together, and the other woman's glamorous appearance was making Amelie feel plain and dumpy rather than bride-like. Smiling through it, she allowed herself to be guided towards a blush velvet chaise longue in the centre of the shop.

Cat and Mum sat down in small cream armchairs either side of her, and Cat bounced her feet up and down excitedly when Sofia presented them with a tray of champagne.

"We are waiting for one more of your party, are we not?" Sofia asked.

Mum nodded mid-sip. "Yes, my sister-in-law. Amelie's Aunt Katie. She should be here any minute now."

Sofia beamed, tilted her head, and waved a hand in the air. "No problem. I will go and fetch the dress, you ladies relax. You are the only ones booked in this morning. We have plenty of time."

As Sofia walked through a small archway at the rear of the shop, Cat widened her eyes. "Wow. This is amazing."

Amelie couldn't help grinning. Finally, she was beginning to feel like a real bride. Until now, organising everything from a different country had made her feel a little detached from it. But today, at last, she was going to have the moment she'd been dreaming of – she would put on her beautiful dress, stand in front of a full-length mirror in a shop that felt like it was full of magic, and be able to truly envisage herself walking down the aisle on her wedding day.

She was on her last mouthful of champagne when the door tinkled and opened inwards. As she looked up, her aunt's smiling face appeared, and Amelie rushed forward to hug her.

"Oh, I'm so glad you could come," she said, squeezing tightly.

"And I'm *so* glad you asked me to." Aunt Katie patted Amelie's hair and then waved at the others.

"We have bubbles…" Cat was offering Katie a glass and as she took it, Sofia reappeared.

In her arms, she was cradling a large cream coloured bag. Amelie held her breath.

"Here it is," Sofia whispered, beckoning Amelie over. Then, to the others, "Give us a few moments, ladies. And we will be back to impress you."

As she stepped into a large, curtained changing room and Sofia hung the dress bag on a hook at the back, Amelie's heart pounded.

"Are you ready?" Sofia had drawn the curtain and was watching Amelie expectantly. Amelie nodded slowly. "Okay…" Sofia reached out and slowly unzipped the bag, then removed a layer of thick plastic wrapping and stepped back.

Amelie swallowed hard. "My goodness," she breathed. "It's stunning."

Sofia clapped her hands and asked Amelie to take off her jeans and blouse. "Now," she said, working on undoing the small delicate buttons at the back of the dress. "This won't be a perfect fit, but I'll re-do your measurements, pin it where it needs to be pinned, and everything will be..." she made a kissing gesture with her fingers, "*just so* for your wedding day."

Amelie's heart was racing and her skin prickled sharply. As Sofia turned her away from the mirror and helped her step into the dress, her breath caught in her throat. "Is it normal to feel this nervous?" she laughed.

"Of course," Sofia smiled. "This is a big moment. Especially as you haven't seen the dress before in person." Finally, she finished fastening Amelie into the dress and stepped back. "There," she said, still smiling. "Now, it's time to look."

Before allowing Amelie to see herself, Sofia opened the curtain and eased her back into the room. The dress was large and heavy, and the high heels Sofia had picked out were making Amelie a little unsteady on her feet.

In front of her, Cat, Katie, and her mother looked up. They were smiling but they didn't speak until Amelie had stepped up onto a small stool in front of them and turned back to look in the mirror.

"It's beautiful," Cat said.

"So lovely," added Katie.

But then Mum asked, tentatively, "Is it what you pictured, Amelie? Do you like it?"

Amelie was studying her reflection. Her strawberry blonde hair, which was piled messily on top of her head and pinned out of the way, the dusting of freckles across the bridge of her nose, and the most wedding-dress-like dress she'd ever seen. Big, white, perfectly smooth, exactly as it had looked in the magazine. Except something was different.

"Amelie?" Mum had walked over and was smiling at her, studying her face.

Amelie started to speak but before she could stop herself, without warning, she began to cry. Not small tears. Big, gasping sobs.

Beside her, Sofia waved her hands and grabbed a box of tissues. "Oh, Amelie. I know it's beautiful but…" She was trying not to grit her teeth. "Be careful, my dear. We don't want mascara stains on the dress."

Amelie shook her head. Her breathing was coming thick and fast, and she felt like she was suffocating. "I need to take it off," she said, reaching behind her for the buttons. "Please, can you undo it? I need to take it off."

Sofia hesitated but when Mum said, "She said she wants to take it off," she hurried over and whisked her back into the changing room.

Stepping out of it, Amelie leaned back against the wall and tried to calm her breathing. "I'm so sorry." She pulled her own clothes back on. Then she ran out of the shop.

13

ROSE

As Amelie hurtled out of the door in a blur, Rose looked at Cat and Katie.

"I'll go after her," Katie said, swiftly following her niece into the bustling plaza outside.

"What the...?" Cat stood up and turned to Sofia, as if the poor woman had somehow caused Amelie's meltdown.

"I don't know what happened," Sofia said, looking slightly tearful herself. "It was exactly the dress she wanted. I can find our emails, but I promise you–"

Rose put her hand on the young woman's arm. "I'm sure it's not the dress. Maybe just last-minute jitters. We'll talk to her, and we'll call to make another appointment."

Sofia nodded then glanced at her diary, which was open on the computer screen near the door. "With only three weeks until the wedding, we need to check her measurements as soon as possible. I have the seamstress booked for early next week."

Rose nodded. "Of course. We'll be in touch." And then she gestured for Cat to follow her, scooped up her handbag, and hurried out to find her daughter.

"Mum, seriously," Cat said as they stepped outside. "What's going on?"

"I don't know," Rose replied quietly, looking at her eldest daughter.

"Do you think she's having second thoughts? Because to be honest, I've never liked Jed very much, and…"

Rose put a finger to Cat's lips and narrowed her eyes at her. "Be careful what you say, darling. We don't know what's happening yet."

Cat pursed her lips as though she was about to disagree. But to Rose's surprise, she didn't answer back. "Sorry. I'm just worried about her. She'd been looking forward to this for weeks…"

"I know." Rose folded her arms in front of her stomach and looked up and down the street. Unable to see her daughter or her sister-in-law, she took out her phone and called Katie, who told her that she'd followed Amelie down to the river.

Setting off in the direction Katie had described, Rose tried to calm the spiky feeling in her chest. But when she saw Amelie, her face blotchy from crying, leaning against Katie's shoulder, the feeling worsened.

"Sweetheart…" She pulled Amelie towards her and kissed her forehead. "Are you all right?"

Taking a deep breath, Amelie straightened herself up and leaned back against the pale stone wall behind them. Mascara was smudged under her eyes and when she wiped them with the back of her hand, the smear got bigger. "I'm so sorry. What did Sofia say?"

Briskly, Cat said, "*Pfft*. Don't worry about that. What's going on? Was it the dress?"

Amelie shook her head, seemingly unable to get any words out, but Katie cut in and answered for her. "Maybe it's all just become a bit much. Weddings can be very stressful." Then, nudging Rose a few feet away from the girls and lowering her voice, she said solemnly, "I think it's just hit her that her dad might not be at the wedding."

Rose blinked hard. She felt like someone had grabbed hold of her insides and was twisting them; Amelie had seemed *okay* with what was going on with Thomas. But, apparently, she was far from it.

Katie squeezed Rose's arm and dipped to meet her eyes. "I'll talk to Thomas," she said. "Okay?"

It was the first time Katie had offered to intervene. Until now, she'd been doing her best to remain neutral, and Rose had refrained from asking her to get involved. But now Rose nodded. For Amelie's sake, someone needed to talk to Thomas.

Looking at Amelie, Rose bit her lower lip. While part of her wanted to hate her husband for what he was putting them all through, at the same time, her heart hadn't quite gotten the message and – as she always had when there was a problem with the children – she suddenly felt desperate to talk to him, to tell him what was going on, to allow him to wrap her in his arms and tell her that everything would work out okay in the end.

Katie put an arm around Rose's shoulders, and they

walked back to where the girls were huddled together, foreheads pressed against one another's, whispering. When Amelie looked up, she smiled a weak smile. "I just... panicked. I think."

Rose reached for her daughter's hand and squeezed it tightly.

"Will Sofia let me go back?" Her eyes had widened. "I can't believe I caused such a scene."

"Of course, she'll let you go back. If you want to?" Rose met Amelie's gaze. "You know, Amelie, your father–"

"I shouldn't have let it get to me." She breathed in sharply. "I've been feeling a little... nervous, I guess. And the thought of Dad not being there, well it just tipped me over the edge. But it's normal to feel nervous, right?" She was speaking quickly and waving her hands as she spoke.

Rose narrowed her eyes, trying to read Amelie's expression to figure out what it was that she wasn't saying. "Yes..." she said slowly. "But–"

"It's just all the planning. You know, doing it from a distance and now trying to tie it all together. And being away from Jed and being back home without Dad or Ethan here. And then seeing the dress..." Amelie smiled, bigger this time, even though it didn't quite reach her eyes. "It's a good dress. Isn't it?"

Furtively, Cat nodded. "It's a great dress." Then she laughed. "Well, I mean, for the thirty seconds we saw you in it, it looked great." She nudged Amelie gently, and Rose was pleased to see Amelie finally smile a real smile at her sister.

But as they made their way back up the sloping cobbled street towards the dress shop, with the girls walking arm-in-arm and Katie by her side, Rose still couldn't shift the knot in her stomach; if Thomas was at home, waiting for her to tell him all about their trip, she would have said to him, *Thomas, I'm worried there's something more going on. I think Amelie's having second thoughts about the wedding. What do I do?*

But Thomas wasn't at home. He'd been gone for six months. And Rose had no idea where he was.

14
THOMAS

THOMAS GOODWIN WOKE BEFORE SUNRISE. As he had every day for the past six months, he slowly sat up, eased his legs out of the small bed in which he had slept, and winced as his feet touched the floor.

The movement sent a jolt of pain through his left leg and up into his hip, but he breathed through it and focussed on the picture he had hung on the bare wooden wall opposite – a photograph of his wife and their four beautiful children. It was taken just three summers ago, but it felt like a lifetime since their smiling faces had surrounded him.

He was opening the shutters and getting ready to pour himself a glass of water when a tap on the door interrupted his routine.

"Tommy? You in there?"

Thomas inhaled sharply and rolled his eyes. In just four steps, he had reached the door of the tiny wooden shepherd's hut in which he had been living and swung it open.

"Katie," he said, looking at the sun, which was only just creeping up over the hills in the distance. "You're early."

"I know." His little sister – he still thought of her as 'little' despite the fact she was now in her mid-sixties – shrugged and then took her hands from behind her back and waved a brown paper bag at him. "But I brought cannoli."

"In that case, you're forgiven." Thomas waved a hand at the two striped deck chairs that he'd set up beneath the canopy at the front of the hut. "Take a seat. I'll bring coffee."

When he returned, Katie had pulled a blanket from the back of one of the chairs and wrapped it around her shoulders. Although the day would be warm, the morning air was yet to shake its night-time chill.

"Thanks," she said, wrapping her hands around the mug he'd offered her.

As Thomas lowered himself into the chair beside her, he tried not to grunt. But he was certain that his facial expression gave away the discomfort he was feeling.

Katie watched him intently, but didn't say anything, and the two of them sat in companionable silence until their mugs were almost empty and the cannoli were demolished. Then finally, she said, "So, how are you?"

"Good." He answered quickly. Too quickly.

"How are you *really*?"

Thomas sighed and rubbed his palms on his thighs. "I'm okay. *Really*."

Katie made a tutting noise at him before turning away and looking out over the valley. "Does it ever strike you as strange?" she said quietly.

Thomas waited for her to explain what she meant.

"That we both ended up here in Italy instead of back home in England."

Thomas rubbed his lightly stubbled jaw with his thumb and forefinger before smiling at her and replying, "Not really. I knew when I moved out here that you'd be hot on my heels."

Katie smiled back – the exact same smile she'd had ever since they were kids, except now with a few extra lines at the corners of her mouth and a hint of grey beneath her blonde highlights. But then her smiled dropped and she looked at him sideways. "Tommy..."

"Uh oh," he said, raising his eyebrows at her. "Must be serious."

Katie tilted her head a little. Her lips were pursed, and she had clasped her hands together in her lap. "Tommy, I came to talk to you about something."

Thomas bit the inside of his cheek. For months, Katie had visited him at the shepherd's hut without saying a word about Rose, or the children, or the mess that Thomas had gotten himself into. She had just come, sat beside him, and left again. And he'd appreciated it more than he could ever have told her. But now, it seemed, she could keep quiet no longer.

"I told you from the beginning that I was going to remain neutral in all of this," she said solemnly. "Rose has been my best friend almost as long as you've been my brother. I introduced the two of you. I've watched you fall in love and live an amazing life together. And the last thing I want to do was take sides. You're my brother. I love you. But I love her and the children too, and I can't–" she stopped, biting back whatever it was that she'd been about to say.

"Katie, I–"

But before he could speak, she raised her palms at him. "It's okay Tommy, I'm not going to tell you that you messed up. I'm not even going to tell you to call Rose."

At the mention of his wife's name, Thomas looked away and scraped his fingers through his greying hair.

Katie ducked to catch hold of his gaze and put her hand firmly on his knee. "But I am going to tell you to call your daughter. Or text her. Or send a carrier pigeon... because Amelie is getting *married* in three weeks. And if you're not there to walk her down the aisle, well then I don't think she will ever forgive you."

Thomas swallowed the lump that had lodged in his throat. Until now, Amelie's wedding had felt like something that would happen 'in the future'. Something he could worry about when he was feeling stronger, both physically and mentally. But suddenly, it had arrived. And he couldn't avoid it any longer.

"I saw her yesterday. We went wedding dress shopping, and she asked me to give you this." Katie produced a small cream envelope from her handbag. "She's been carrying it around for months."

Thomas closed his eyes. Guilt swept over him like a feeling of seasickness.

"You *are* coming, aren't you?" Katie wasn't taking her eyes away from his face.

"Yes," he said, hoarsely. "Of course, I am."

"Good. Then tell her."

Thomas rested his elbows on his knees and rubbed his hands over his face as if the gesture might scrub away some of the anxiety on his skin. "How should I...?" He looked at his sister. "I haven't spoken to any of them since I left. Not the kids. Or Rose. I let them know I was okay, but since then…"

"I know," Katie replied gently. Then she reached into her handbag and took out a small notepad. "If you don't feel like you can call, write a note."

Thomas stood up, took the notepad, and clasped it tightly between his fingers. Pacing up and down through the long grass in front of the hut, he looked out at the valley beyond and inhaled a long forceful breath. He let the air fill his lungs, pushed the oxygen through his body, down into his limbs, and closed his eyes. When he opened them again, he asked Katie for a pen.

A few minutes later, he handed her back the notebook. He had written just a few lines. Not nearly enough. But a start, at least.

"Okay. Good." Katie stood up and put her hand on his shoulder. "I'm proud of you, Tommy."

Thomas looked away from her, blinking back the moisture that was scratching at his eyes. Then he chuckled dolefully. "You know," he said, "I'm pretty glad you followed me out here all those years ago – looks like I'll never be too old to need my sister's wisdom."

Katie smiled at him, wrinkling her nose. "I love you too, big brother."

15

AMELIE

AMELIE REACHED DOWN and patted Rupert's mane. The feeling of his coarse blond hair beneath her fingers calmed the tightness in her chest, and as she rode him slowly into the shade of the trees, she leaned down and whispered, "Thank you, boy. This was exactly what I needed today."

As if he understood, Rupert moved his lips over his teeth and made a *snuff* sound, then he drew to a stop beside the river and let Amelie dismount.

Looping his reins loosely around the thick twisted branch of a nearby tree, Amelie encouraged Rupert to drink and sat down beside him on a smooth boulder. The creek had always been her favourite part of the river; shallow enough for paddling, and cool, but if you rode upstream a little it became deeper and wider. About an hour's ride away from the ranch, it was somewhere the guests rarely came to unless on an organised trek, and she had consulted the diary before leaving so she was certain she wouldn't be interrupted.

From the small backpack she'd brought with her, she took out a battered paperback edition of *Little Women* and opened it to the last page she'd read. Before she'd even started reading, however, she turned back to the beginning. Inside the front cover was an inscription.

For my little women. I am so proud of you both. Love,
Dad xxx

Amelie pressed the book to her chest. She had carried it with her on almost every trip she'd taken for over twenty years and had read both the inscription and the story so many times that she knew them by heart. Cat had a copy too, with the same message, although Amelie wasn't sure that Cat had treasured hers quite as much; she'd never been as sentimental as Amelie.

"Good book?"

Amelie blinked and looked up. Skye was walking towards her and, perhaps because she was sitting down, she marvelled at how tall he was.

A smile fluttered to her lips, and she closed the cover. "Very. Although, I haven't actually got very far. I've only been here a few minutes."

Skye paused. He'd been riding his favourite horse, Shadow, but was now standing with her reins in his hand. "Sorry," he said, gesturing back towards the path. "We'll go."

"Oh, no. I didn't mean it like that." Amelie patted a spare rock. "Sit down. Honestly, it's nice to see you. Did you know I'd be here?"

As Skye sat down, and Shadow nudged up beside Rupert,

he kicked off his boots and dipped his toes into the water. "Had a hunch," he said, his lips twitching into a smile. "I haven't seen you much the last few days. So, I thought maybe you were seeking some solitude."

"And you decided to come interrupt me?" Amelie jokingly pressed her shoulder into Skye's upper arm.

"Yeah," he said. "I did."

"Well, you're right." Amelie tapped her fingers on the cover of the book she was holding. "I've been feeling a bit – off kilter. The dress fitting was a disaster and after that…" Amelie trailed off; she wasn't sure why she'd been avoiding Skye. But she knew she had been. Since the incident at Sofia's store, she'd felt agitated and grumpy. So, she'd spent the past two days staying out of everyone's way and trying to muddle her way through her own tangle of thoughts.

Skye nodded and reached into his backpack to take out a bottle of water. He took a long, slow swig from it. Then, just when Amelie thought he might change the subject, he asked, "A disaster?"

Amelie breathed in and held the air in her chest for longer than usual. Sunlight was dripping through the trees above them, casting dappled freckles on the water's edge. She focussed on them instead of the tight, prickly feeling in her chest, then breathed out. "The dress was lovely. But…" She was almost wincing as she spoke. Bending her knee so that her foot rested on the rock, she wriggled her toes. She'd been going over and over what had happened, but still couldn't figure out why she had panicked, run away, and spent most of the afternoon crying instead of feeling how she was supposed to feel – on top of the world.

"We don't have to talk about it," Skye said, looking out across the water.

Almost laughing, Amelie waved her hands in the air. "The thing is, I want to talk about it. But I don't know what to say. I just... panicked. I put on the dress and it was beautiful. It was big, and white, and bride-like. But I didn't feel *joy* when I looked at it. I didn't feel like a bride. I felt like some imposter playing dress-up." She shrugged, watching the shallow water flow smoothly over the riverbed in front of her. "And then I started to think about the church, and the guests, and..." Amelie looked down at the book she was holding. "And about walking down the aisle without my dad there to steady me. And I just–"

"Freaked out?" Skye met her eyes and smiled.

"Yeah." Amelie tried to laugh. "Quite a bit."

"Well, that's okay. We all freak out sometimes."

Amelie tilted her head and took in Skye's broad frame and square jaw. She couldn't imagine him ever freaking out. About anything. "Even you?"

Skye frowned at her and looked down at himself as though he saw a very different version from the one she saw. "Definitely me."

They held one another's gaze. Amelie gestured to the book she was holding. "Mum and Dad adopted me when I was four. I don't remember much of the time before that, but I know things were... not good."

Skye was watching her carefully, and Amelie was aware that she hadn't ever spoken to him about her life before the ranch. Mostly, this was because she didn't remember enough of it to speak about it. But it was also because she had learned a long time ago that it could make people uncomfortable – as if they weren't quite sure what to say or what to ask. Jed, in particular, hadn't been very receptive to hearing about Amelie's early years, about what her life had been like before she was placed into care and adopted into the Goodwin family. He'd asked her once whether she knew about any family history of genetic disease or inheritable conditions, presumably because he was worried about any future children they might have. But when she told him there had been nothing mentioned in her adoption files, he'd seemed satisfied with that. And he hadn't asked her about it since.

"From the day I arrived at the ranch," Amelie said, "I idolised my dad. Thomas Goodwin. This big, kind, smiling man who was just the total opposite of the people I'd known before."

"It must be hard," Skye said tentatively, "feeling that way about him, but seeing how much he's hurt your mum?"

Amelie nodded. She had been flicking the corner of the book's front cover with her index finger and now opened it and passed it to Skye. "When I was eight, Dad was called back to England just before Christmas. Aunt Katie's husband was ill, and she was in pieces. We were devastated – Cat and the boys and me. We were young, and we were more upset by the idea of him not being around at Christmas time than by Uncle Jerry being ill. But Mum insisted he go. So, it ended up just the five of us."

Skye had opened the book and was reading the inscription.

"On Christmas morning, as always, there were stockings hanging on the fireplace and we had Nonna's *huge* breakfast spread. But we said we'd wait until Dad came home to do presents. So, we went out to see to the horses, had lunch, played games... the usual stuff." Amelie smiled as memories of family Christmases danced through her head. "Then just before bed, Mum presented us each with a special gift that Dad had left for us. Cat and I got *Little Women,* and the boys got *Treasure Island.* I spent the next few days devouring every word, and when he came home on New Year's Eve, I felt like my heart would burst." Amelie bit her lower lip. "It was the first time the family had been separated since I'd come to the ranch, and it was awful. So awful. But reading that book made me feel safer, warmer, like everything would be okay."

Amelie was beginning to cry, and she knew there was no way she could stop it; since her father had left the ranch, disappeared into the ether with not a word to any of them, she had tried so hard to pretend that it wasn't affecting her. But it was. "I just never thought that *he* would abandon me," she whispered.

Skye took her hand in his. His fingers were warm, and he squeezed hers lightly in his palm.

"It's ridiculous. I'm almost thirty years old. It's Mum who should be upset, not me." She sniffed and wiped at her eyes with the back of her spare hand. "But being here without him... it's too strange. It's not right."

Tweaking his index finger under her chin, so she looked up at him, Skye smiled softly. "You have every right to be upset. This is your family, and it's changed. This is the first place where you were truly looked after, and safe, and loved. And you're still all of those things, but the dynamics have shifted." Skye wrapped his arm around her shoulders and pulled her closer, so that her head was resting on his shoulder. "Getting married is a big deal. There's a lot going on. And it's completely normal to be feeling *whatever* you're feeling about it. Okay?"

Amelie smiled weakly but as she sat up, a stubborn tear rolled down her cheek.

Skye caught it with his thumb and smiled back. "Seriously, Amelie. It's going to be okay."

For a long moment, she found herself unable to look away. Skye's thumb was resting just below her ear, and his vivid green eyes were reflecting the golden freckles on the water. She felt herself lean into him. But then, behind her, Rupert scuffed the ground loudly and let out a disgruntled *humph* sound that made them both laugh.

"I think he's ready for the swim I promised him," Amelie said, shuffling back on her rock and tucking *Little Women* back into her bag.

"Swim?" Skye's eyes widened. "Now, *that* is a good idea."

16

ROSE

FOR NEARLY TWO WEEKS, Rose had allowed Alec Anderson to observe the daily happenings and routines of the ranch. He had risen early, accompanied her to the stables, and gotten stuck in. He'd looked carefully at the roster of which horses would be trekking, which were on rest days, and which were being used for beginners' lessons in the paddocks closest to the house. He had listened intently as Rose had explained how Jean allocated horses to the guests based on each person's weight, experience, personality, and which particular routes they would take on their treks. And he had marvelled at the number of volunteers who came every summer to work in exchange for food, accommodation, and free riding.

"Thomas started the volunteer programme years ago, and it's gone from strength to strength." Rose was splashing water on her face from the trough in the yard and sighed as it trickled down her neck.

It was midday and hot. Too hot to be out in the sun.

"A fantastic way of keeping costs down," Alec said as they walked back up to the house.

Rose tipped her head from side to side. "It is, but it also allows us to spend a little more on hiring the best people to teach and to lead the more adventurous treks."

Alec nodded approvingly. He seemed irritatingly impervious to the hot weather, whereas Rose – who had lived in Italy for half her life, but who still carried her English proclivity for a cooler climate – felt as if she was melting.

As they reached the main house, Alec nodded at the veranda. It was dotted with guests, who were enjoying large jugs of iced tea and plates full to the brim with Nonna's lunch time offerings. "Is this the busiest it gets?"

"Pretty much. We're coming to the end of the high season. It usually stretches until the end of September, but then the weather becomes a little more unpredictable. By the end of October, we'll be down to about a quarter capacity. And then we traditionally take November through to the end of February to do essential maintenance, give the horses a break, and train up new recruits."

"New horses?"

Rose nodded. "Although, this year, I haven't..." She trailed off, hoping that Alec understood the reason she hadn't invested in any new stock this year.

In the kitchen, Rose handed Alec a glass of water. "I'm going to freshen up. You should help yourself to some lunch."

Alec nodded but before Rose could turn and leave, he blurted. "Rose, before you go..."

Rose blew a puff of air up into her face. She really did need a shower.

"I've come to a decision."

Her mouth dropped open and then closed again. She had not expected this. Not now. Not so informally.

"I'm going to offer you the asking price for the business."

Rose steadied herself against the kitchen cabinets. She had pictured this moment and how she would react a million times. And yet, now that it was here, she was struggling to feel much of anything at all. On autopilot, she heard herself say, "That's fantastic, Alec."

"So, you'll accept? Once I've drawn up the paperwork, of course."

Rose nodded as Alec reached out to shake her hand. "Yes." She forced a smile to her lips. "Yes, I'll accept."

"And Thomas?" Alec was watching her closely. By now, he knew enough to know that she and Thomas were not in regular contact.

Rose released a slow, shaky breath. "He will too."

After excusing herself from the kitchen, Rose walked upstairs in a daze and sat down on the end of her bed. She had agreed to sell the ranch. Alec had offered exactly what she'd asked. And she'd said yes. In a few months, *Heart of the Hills* would belong to Alec Anderson.

The magnitude of it made her feel like she was swimming underwater, her surroundings distorted and hazy and out of focus. Where would she go? What would she *do*?

What had seemed like a watertight plan a few days ago was now causing a tsunami of questions and doubts to hurtle through her mind, and she felt the urgent need to vomit.

Rushing to the bathroom, Rose knelt in front of the toilet and held back her hair. But, almost as soon as the feeling had come, it disappeared. Breathless, she leaned against the cool tiles beside the sink and brought her knees up to her chin.

She and Thomas were too old to find a new form of income. So, whatever was left after paying off Thomas' debts would be their lot. Everything. It would have to last another twenty or thirty years. And, when you put it like that, it suddenly didn't seem very much at all.

As Rose stepped into the shower and let a stream of cold water pummel her shoulders, she briefly wondered whether they could buy somewhere small and run it as a B&B. She pictured herself and Thomas cooking breakfast, welcoming guests, living a quieter and simpler life. Perhaps somewhere near *Lucca*, where Katie lived. But then, the image of Thomas began to quiver. And he disappeared.

There was no more Thomas. He had left her. They were no longer a happy young couple bursting with passion and ideas. Their marriage had been tainted. And wiping out the hurt Thomas had caused would not be as straightforward as wiping out the money he owed.

Wrapping a towel around herself, Rose padded back into the bedroom and reached for her phone. When Thomas first left, she promised herself that she wouldn't put Katie in the middle. The two of them had been friends almost their entire lives. But Thomas was Katie's big brother, and so Rose vowed never to ask her to do anything that would force her to choose who to be loyal to. Allowing Katie to talk to Thomas about Amelie's wedding was one thing – roping her into the potential sale of the ranch was another.

But Rose was out of options.

Katie, I never wanted to ask you this, but I need to speak to Thomas. Do you know where he is?

Three little dots appeared, disappeared, then reappeared. And finally, her friend replied: *Yes. Do you need his number or his address?*

Rose paused with her thumbs above the keyboard. Then she breathed in and typed: *Address. This is something I need to talk to him about in person.*

17
AMELIE

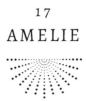

A LITTLE WAY upstream from where they'd talked, Amelie and Skye came to a deeper part of the river. The water was slow moving, and there were fewer rocks. So, they left the horses paddling by the bank and waded in.

Amelie had come prepared and was wearing a striped navy swimming costume beneath her clothes. But Skye had only his shorts and t-shirt, so strode out into the water fully clothed.

When the river reached waist-height, they both began to swim.

"Feeling better?" Skye asked, swimming up beside her.

Amelie closed her eyes and breathed deeply, allowing the scent and sounds of the forest to melt into her skin. "I should have done this days ago." Then, opening them, she asked, "Why is it so different? Swimming out here rather than in the pool?"

"Because out here, we're alone." Skye was watching her,

and a smile that she hadn't seen before darted across his lips. "Nothing but birds, and squirrels, and those two." Skye gestured to the horses and smiled again. But something in his voice made Amelie look away.

Alone. They were alone. Since she'd arrived at the ranch, she'd seen Skye almost every day. She enjoyed his company. She looked forward to seeing him. And back on the rocks, she was certain they'd had… what? A moment? A frisson? An almost-something?

Sensing that the air between them had changed, Skye cleared his throat and began to slowly sweep his arms back and forth through the water. "So, when's Jed arriving?"

Amelie felt the need to look at her watch, even though it didn't display a date. "Next week."

"Ah. Not long then."

"No. Not long."

"I'm looking forward to meeting him."

"You are?" Amelie studied Skye's features for a hint of sarcasm but found none.

"Sure." Skye said lightly, then nodded towards a bend in the river up ahead. "I'm going to swim for a bit. You want to…?"

"I think I'll stay here," Amelie replied. "Keep an eye on the horses." But as Skye swam away, she wasn't watching the horses; she was watching him. And trying to ignore the fierce pulsing sensation that took hold of her chest as she realised that perhaps her father's absence wasn't the only thing causing her to feel anxious about the wedding.

Amelie paddled for a few more minutes, then retreated to the riverbank to dry off. There were fewer trees here, and she lay back on the grassy floor as if she was sunbathing at the beach. When she sat back up, she had lost sight of Skye, but it wasn't long before he appeared from around the bend. As the water became shallower, he stood up and walked towards her. His clothes were wet, his shirt clinging to his shoulders and causing Amelie to turn away. "You're drenched," she said, lifting her hand to shield her eyes from the sun as she finally looked at him.

Skye smiled – the same cheeky smile he'd had when he was a boy – and shook his arms like a dog trying to free its coat of moisture after an impromptu dip. "I'll dry off on the way back," he said, walking over to Shadow and starting to ready her for the return journey.

Reluctant to leave, Amelie stood up and pulled her clothes on top of her now almost-dry swimming costume. Rubbing Rupert's nose as she prepared to climb up into his saddle, she noticed Skye wringing moisture from the corner of his t-shirt and shook her head at him. "You know, most guys would have just ditched the shirt *pre*-swim," she said, Cat's voice in her head adding, *And isn't it a shame he didn't?!*

Skye looked over at her and brushed the front of his shirt with the palms of his hands.

Swinging up into Rupert's saddle, Amelie raised her eyebrows at him. "You don't strike me as the body-conscious type. Were you trying to spare my blushes?"

She was almost flirting, and she knew it. She could hear how her words sounded but, somehow, she couldn't stop them; she liked how she and Skye were with each other and there was no harm in it, was there? They were friends. Friends who exchanged playful banter. Plenty of people had friends like that – and just because she was getting married, it didn't mean she should cloister herself away or make things awkward between them.

As she smiled at him, she expected Skye to respond with a witty remark or for him to jokingly flex his muscles at her. But something different flitted across his face – a kernel of thought that she couldn't interpret – and he simply said, "Something like that."

An hour later, they were almost back at the ranch. For most of the journey, they had been reliving the summer, when they were about fourteen years old, that had ended up blighted by unexpected thunderstorms for the whole of July. That summer, the four Goodwin children and Skye had spent weeks on end playing board games and chasing one another around the ranch house, causing chaos and getting under everyone's feet, and it remained one of Amelie's fondest memories of when Skye and his parents had visited.

But as they broke out of the forest and began trekking down the sloping hills towards the fields on the outer edge of the property, Skye became quiet. Amelie was about to ask if he was all right when, so quietly she almost missed it, he said, "I have some scars."

Amelie looked across at him and, as if the small horse could read the situation, Rupert slowed down to match Shadow's pace. "Scars?"

Skye sat up a little straighter in his saddle and let the reins hang loose in his hands. He wasn't looking at her. His statement was so incongruous with their previous conversation that, at first, Amelie wasn't sure what to say. But then she remembered her jibe about him taking his shirt off and mentally kicked herself in the shin... how could she have been so insensitive?

"From your time in the Army?" Her eyes moved to the indentation on his forehead.

Skye nodded. "Before I left."

Amelie nudged Rupert closer to Shadow and reached out to lightly touch Skye's leg. Guilt tugged at her chest. "I'm sorry. I shouldn't have made fun of you, I was..."

"It's fine, Amelie, really." He finally looked at her. "I wasn't trying to make you feel bad. I just wanted you to know."

"Okay," she said, her hand still resting on his leg. "But just so that *you* know... you don't have to hide your scars from me."

Skye blinked at her, looked down at his fingers, then nodded. "Ditto," he said.

18
ROSE

Two Days Later

ROSE ASKED Alec to stop at the edge of the wood. "I'll walk from here," she breathed. "I know the way."

"You've been here before?" Alec looked ominously at the densely set trees in front of them.

They were on the edge of a forest that was a long, winding, three-hour drive away from the ranch. "Thomas and I honeymooned here," Rose replied.

Alec's eyebrows twitched, as if he was trying not to seem surprised. "Oh."

"The hut belongs to an old friend. He was the ranch's vet a long time ago." Rose breathed in and tried to relax her shoulders; she'd never been Rossi the vet's biggest fan, but he'd been good to them over the years and, clearly, in Thomas' hour of need he had come through once again. "I should have guessed Thomas would come here," she said, wondering whether it would have made any difference even if she had known where her husband was all these months.

"If you need me..." Alec gestured to his phone. "Just call."

"I will. If I have a signal." Rose was already opening the door. "And if not, I'll come fetch you."

Alec nodded solemnly. He still looked deeply uncomfortable about Rose doing this alone but, despite how much she appreciated him coming along in case Thomas wanted to ask questions, she was sincerely hoping that Alec wouldn't be needed. Surely, Thomas would understand that she would never *ever* suggest that they sell the ranch if it wasn't the only option. Surely, he wouldn't fight her on it. Not after everything he'd put the family through these past eighteen months.

Trying to remind herself that the man she was about to come face to face with was her husband – the one person in the world who she knew better than anyone else – Rose flexed her fingers to release some tension, then marched off through the trees.

As she headed down the thin, well-trodden path that led through the undergrowth, the air was cool. Looking back, Alec's rental car was already almost invisible, and Rose vividly remembered parking in that exact spot nearly thirty years ago.

In front of her, a mirage from another time, she saw two shimmering figures – youthful versions of herself and Thomas, arm-in-arm, smiling and giggling as they searched for the place where they would spend their modest seven-day honeymoon.

Rose stopped. She was close to the edge of the wood. In a few paces, she would burst out into the meadow that belonged to Rossi's family. With its sweeping views of the valley, its gold-tipped grasses, and the babbling brook that ran through its middle, it was the perfect romantic hide-out.

All those years ago, having barely left the ranch since they met, fell in love, and got married, this spot had felt like paradise. But before she lost herself in the memory of it, Rose took a deep breath and stepped out into the open.

Instantly, the sun warmed her cheeks. She narrowed her eyes at it and lowered her sunglasses as she approached the small wooden hut that sat proudly in the centre of the meadow.

Out front were two striped deckchairs, a fire pit, and a sun canopy that was rolled half-way back to the cabin. The door was closed. Rose looked at her watch. It was midday, and she had no idea whether that meant that her husband was likely to be inside or not. She reached for her wedding band and twisted it, round and round, unable to move any closer.

Finally, as if she had willed it to happen just by staring at it, the door opened.

Rose cleared her throat, straightened her shoulders, and tried to fix a steady expression on her face. But as soon as she saw Thomas emerge from inside, she felt herself waver.

He was looking down at his feet, walking slowly forward, and yawning as if he'd just woken from a long nap. His face had a familiar soft, crumpled look to it. And there was a hole in the toe of his left sock that made her want to roll her eyes. Taking him in, in those few brief moments before he noticed her, Rose felt instantly light-headed; emotions and memories, and words that she'd wanted to say for far too long, formed a hot, swirling pool at the base of her stomach.

But then his eyes lifted.

"Rose?" Hearing her name on his lips was like coming home, but she refused to let what she was feeling show on her face. She was glad she was wearing sunglasses.

"Thomas," she replied, folding her arms in front of her chest. "I asked Katie where you were staying."

Thomas nodded as if he was simply surprised that she hadn't asked sooner, then descended the steps towards her. "I'm glad you did," he said. "I've been wanting to..." He looked away, scraped his fingers through his still-dark hair, and cleared his throat. When he looked back, she was almost certain that his eyes were shimmering with moisture.

"I came because I need to talk to you about something." Rose had written a script in her head, and she needed to stick to it. If she allowed herself to ask how he was or talk about the children, she might never say what she needed to say.

"Can I get you a drink? It's quite a drive. Coffee? Tea?"

"No, thanks." She sat down in one of the deck chairs and gestured for him to do the same. Feeling brave, she pushed her sunglasses on top of her head.

"I wrote to Amelie. About the wedding." Thomas had sat down beside her and was leaning his forearms on his thighs, fingers laced together, watching her.

Rose raised her eyebrows; she didn't know that. "It's not the wedding I'm here to talk about, Thomas."

"It's not?" He was frowning, and Rose noticed his jaw twitch the way it always did when he was afraid that she was going to reprimand him for something. It almost made her want to smile; even now, at seventy-two years old, her husband looked like a frightened schoolboy when he thought she was going to be cross with him. Probably, that was why he'd been unable to tell her about the gambling, and the money, and the debt – because even though anger was barely ever her first reaction to a problem, he had a pathological fear of upsetting her.

Rose reached for her handbag – the large leather one that he'd bought her from a market in Florence. From it, she took the folder of information she'd prepared – breakdowns of their finances, forecasts for the next year, and a copy of the draft contract Alec had drawn up. She handed it to her husband but before he had a chance to open it, she said, "Wait until I'm gone before you look through it. Let me explain first, then..." She nodded slowly to show him she was serious. "Then read it."

Thomas' fingers tightened on the brown cardboard file. "Rose... please. Can we talk about this?"

Rose narrowed her eyes. Had Katie told him...?

"I can't sign them." Thomas tapped the file with his index finger. When he looked up at her, his features were arranged in a way that she couldn't quite interpret. "I can't sign divorce papers, Rose," he said hoarsely. "I still love you. No matter what, I love you."

Thomas reached for her hand, but Rose pulled back and looked up at the sky. She wanted to laugh because perhaps it would release some of the tension that was gripping her chest. Instead, she stood up and turned around, bracing her hands on her hips and looking away from the cabin.

When she turned back, Thomas had opened the file and

was tracing his finger down the writing on the first page. "They're not divorce papers, Thomas. They're—"

"The ranch?" Thomas' words came out low and gruff as he skimmed the letter that Rose had written. "You want to sell the ranch?"

Without thinking, Rose leaned forward and snatched back the file, sweeping it off Thomas' lap and tucking it under her arm. "This is for when I'm gone. To help you... I need to explain first—"

"Explain that you want to sell our home?" Thomas stood up and walked towards her.

"Of course, I don't *want* to. But, Thomas, I'm out of ideas." Rose tried to soften her voice, to make him see that this wasn't an act of revenge or a spur-of-the-moment decision but something she was doing for their family. And something she didn't want to have to do alone.

"Right now, we're covering the repayments on what we owe. But over the winter season, it's going to be tough. We'll have to cut back on the maintenance we usually do. Next year, we won't be able to afford a full staff. We'll have to let some of the horses go. Next summer, we won't be able to run at full capacity. And things will continue to get worse..." Rose held out the folder, gripping it with both hands, willing him to see past the fear and anger and shame he was feeling and to understand what she was saying. "It's all in here. All the workings out. But Thomas, if we sell now, we can repay what we owe and there will be enough left for us to start new lives. If we wait, hang on until the eleventh hour... well, then the ranch won't be an attractive prospect. We'll struggle to sell and if we do, it'll be at a rock-bottom price. We'll be left with nothing. We won't even be able to finish paying Ethan's school fees."

Rose let her words hang in the air between them. Thomas held out his hand, and she placed the file back into it. His face had been eerily still as he listened to her. Apart from his cheeks beginning to flush, there was no sign he had even heard her. After a long silence, he released a hollow laugh and muttered, "I think divorce might have been easier to swallow."

At that, Rose felt her legs waver. She'd always known that the horses came first. She knew when she met him that the ranch, and the business, and the animals were his passion. It was part of why she fell for him all those years ago. But was Thomas really saying that ending their marriage would be less painful than selling their business?

As if he could hear her thoughts, he stepped closer and added quietly, "I didn't mean it like that. I meant..."

"It doesn't matter."

"Of course, it does."

"No, it doesn't." Rose took a deep breath. Years ago, maybe even as recently as six months ago, she would have bitten her tongue and walked away. She would have been reluctant to say what she felt because her instinct was always to protect and to nurture. And because no matter how much pain someone had caused her, she always – whether or not she wanted to – saw the situation from both sides of the ravine. Not just her own.

But standing in the meadow where she had, nearly thirty years ago, spent her honeymoon – and looking at the man she had loved for over a quarter of a century – Rose simply couldn't do it. She couldn't swallow down her feelings any longer.

Meeting Thomas' eyes, she put her hand firmly on his forearm. A jolt of electricity flickered through her skin, but she ignored it. "What matters now, Thomas, is that it's time for you to be a grown-up," she said. "You messed up. You did something stupid, and instead of staying to face up to it, or even talking to me about it, you ran away."

Thomas looked at her hand and put his on top of it.

Looking at their surroundings instead of at him, Rose continued. "You came out here, and you spent time healing yourself, working on being whole again, getting well. And that's great. I'm pleased for you." She realised that tears had started to fall down her cheeks and wiped them with the back of her free hand. "But while you were doing that, I was at home dealing with the mess you left behind. I didn't get to quit. I didn't get to walk away. No one gave me that option. So, I did the best I could. I did the best I could to save our home. But now I'm telling you, Thomas, that there is nothing else to be done."

"Rose..."

Rose tugged herself away from him and adjusted her bag on her shoulder, preparing herself to leave. "Alec Anderson has made us an offer. It's a good one. All the details are there, and I'd rather sell to someone we know – who will look after the place and love it the way we have – than to some faceless corporation who'll turn it into a boutique hotel or a luxury riding school."

"Alec Anderson?"

"I haven't told the children yet. I wanted to wait until I'd spoken to you, but Alec needs a decision by the end of the month and – ideally – if you agree, then I think we should tell the kids after the wedding, while they're all together."

Thomas' mouth dropped open a little, but no sound came out.

Rose inhaled slowly. She had said what she came to say. Now, all she needed to do was force herself to walk away from Thomas. She had gone just a few paces when she stopped and looked back. Thomas was standing in the exact same spot but then he broke into a jog. A clumsy, slow jog that left him wincing after the smallest of distances.

"If I sign this, what about us?"

Rose tilted her head. "Us?"

"Yes, Rose..." Thomas took both of her hands between his and looked into her eyes. "What about *us*?"

19

AMELIE

"Skye?" Amelie was walking towards Skye and Alec's cabin, waving to catch his attention even though he was facing away from her. It was mid-afternoon, stiflingly hot, and the supposedly cool and floaty top she'd chosen that morning was now clinging to the small of her back.

Hearing her voice, Skye turned around and stopped in the middle of the path. "Hey," he said, waiting until she'd caught up with him before continuing. "I was just heading back to freshen up. I rode up into the hills with Ben this morning. It was great but..." He gestured to his clothes, which were coated in a thin layer of the sandy dust that covered the trails to the north of the property.

"Ah, I wondered where you were." Amelie looked down at her shoes. "I came to find you this morning to see if you wanted to head out together. But I guess you'd already gone."

Since their swim a few days ago, it now seemed to be Skye's turn to avoid her. She wasn't sure whether it was because of their strange moment on the rocks, or because he'd told her about his scars and wished he hadn't, or for some other reason entirely. But it was bothering Amelie. Waiting for him to answer, she realised she was fidgeting up and down on the balls of her feet.

Skye rubbed the back of his neck. He looked warm. "Sorry. Ben offered–"

"Oh, no need to say sorry. You're on holiday. You're supposed to be having fun." Amelie smiled, then reminded herself why she'd come to find him in the first place. "But listen… how much do you know about donkeys?"

Skye frowned. "Donkeys?"

"You know, like horses? But smaller."

"I–"

Shaking her head at her own sarcasm, Amelie continued hurriedly, "It's just, I'm a bit worried about Dot. He's not his usual self. Mum asked me to check in on him while she's away for the night and..."

Skye's eyes twinkled. He looked like he was considering saying something witty in response, but then his features settled and, rolling up his sleeves, he said, "Okay. Let's go take a look."

"He's fine, maybe just a little too much sun."

"Donkeys can get sunstroke?" Amelie patted Dot between the ears and lowered her forehead, pressing it against his nose.

"Something like that," Skye said. "Some shade, plenty of

water, and no long walks on the beach, and he should be just fine."

Amelie smiled, and when she looked up, she realised that Skye was watching her.

"Don't you miss the animals?" he asked as they started to walk back up to the ranch house. "When you're in London?"

Thinking of her and Jed's sparse apartment, and their view of the high-rise office buildings beyond it, Amelie nodded. "I do, yes. The most wildlife I see on a daily basis is the pigeons on the balcony."

"I hate pigeons," Skye said bitterly.

Amelie laughed. "Me too."

"So, why settle there? Was it Jed? Or the job?"

At the mention of her job, Amelie began to fiddle with the hair tie on her wrist. "Oh, it wasn't Jed. We only met a year ago." She purposefully didn't look at Skye to see whether he'd raised his eyebrows at that information. "No, I wanted to work in publishing. London's a good place for that. I was pretty career focussed until the beginning of this year."

"And now you're not?"

Amelie shrugged. Why was he asking such difficult questions? "Things change," she said, swiftly diverting the conversation away from her own lack of employment and towards Skye's. "What about you? What will you do after your vacation's over?"

Neither Skye nor Alec seemed to be in a hurry to get back to America. Looking away from her and up into the trees, Skye tweaked the collar of his pale checked shirt and Amelie noticed his jaw twitch. "Guess I'm still figuring that one out."

Amelie nodded, and her mind wandered. She was about to ask Skye if he thought it was odd that their parents had disappeared on an overnight 'business' trip together, even if they were stopping over at Aunt Katie's, when a shrill shrieking sound from up near the house made her jump.

She could just about make out Cat's silhouette on the veranda. She was waving madly, and as they drew closer Amelie realised why.

"Ethan?!" Amelie left Skye behind and ran to throw her arms around her baby brother.

"You knew I was arriving today, right?" As Ethan spoke, a slightly American twang laced his accent, and he patted Amelie's back as she squeezed him tightly.

"I did. But it's still flipping amazing to see your face," Amelie said. Turning to Cat, she asked, "Where's Ben? Isn't he here?"

"Sorting something with a group of angry Brits," said Cat. "They're not keen on the horses we've allocated them." Her sister rolled her eyes. "If I were him, I'd tell them to go stay somewhere else."

"But Ben's too *gentile* for that," Ethan said snippily.

"Indeed."

While Cat agreed with Ethan, Amelie flinched – she'd noticed the scratchiness in Ethan's tone, and it bothered her. It wasn't like him to be so scathing of his twin brother and, suddenly, she was determined to fix whatever was going on between the two of them.

"Well…" Amelie put her arm around Ethan's shoulders. "Mum's away tonight, so it's just us lot as your welcome party, I'm afraid." She turned and gestured to Skye, who shook hands with Ethan and said, "Good to see you, buddy."

"Away? Away where?" Ethan flopped down onto the porch swing and crossed his ankle over his knee so that his skinny legs were on show.

Amelie glanced at Cat, then Skye. "She went to Florence with Alec."

"Florence? Cool. Love it there." Ethan pushed a pair of sunglasses up the bridge of his nose and leaned his head back like he was about to take a nap.

"They're staying overnight," Amelie added.

"With Aunt Katie," Cat said pointedly as she down beside Ethan. "Alec had business in Florence and Mum went along to look for 'mother of the bride' shoes."

Next to one another, despite not being biologically related, Cat and Ethan looked remarkably similar. Examining them, Amelie decided it was their mannerisms; they each had a carefree aura about them that neither she nor Ben had seemed to master.

"Okay, so what's the plan? Get drunk and party? Or are we too old for that?" Ethan grinned at the three of them then shook his head. "Yeah, you're right. Too old. Maybe food, board games, and an early night?"

"Or perhaps something in between?" Cat nudged him in the ribs with her elbow.

"Board games *and* drinks?" Ethan nodded at her. "Now you're talking."

20
ROSE

KATIE GREETED them with an enormous smile and kisses on the cheek. She had met Alec only once, maybe a decade ago, but hadn't hesitated to agree that the pair of them should stop over with her in *Lucca* on their way home.

Ushering them inside, she told them to leave their overnight bags by the door and immediately took them through the house and into her small walled courtyard. "I'll be back with tea," she said.

As if he could sense that Rose needed a few moments alone to recalibrate, Alec offered to help her and followed Katie inside.

Alone, Rose walked towards the small swimming pool at the rear of the courtyard and kicked off her shoes. Her feet were hot and, a habit her body had picked up some time in the last five or six years, after a couple of hours travelling her ankles had become puffy and uncomfortable. Sitting down, she dipped her toes into the water and kept going until it was midway up her calves.

She hadn't answered Thomas and, even after the two-hour drive from the cabin to Lucca, his question was still playing on a loop inside her mind: *What about us? What about us? What about us?*

In truth, since Thomas left her, she hadn't allowed herself to think about the future. She hadn't imagined a joyful reunion. And neither had she imagined them going their separate ways, living separate lives, meeting other people. Perhaps because she didn't know where he was or what he was thinking, she had focussed solely on the ranch. The day-to-day and the immediate problem at hand – their finances.

She still loved him. She still *felt* married to him. But seeing him in the meadow had caused so many conflicting emotions that her head was still spinning from it.

"In a way," she'd said to Alec as they drove along the highway, "he's still the same person he's always been. He looks the same. He sounds the same. And I'm pretty sure he loves me the same."

"But?" Alec had said, reading the tone of her voice.

"But he lied to me. For months. And then he left me." Rose had swallowed hard and blinked quickly at the roof of the car to stop herself from crying. "Even if I could forgive him for it... how do I forget?"

Of course, Alec hadn't been able to answer her. And now, replaying their conversation as she let Katie's swimming pool nurse her legs, she felt a little embarrassed about opening up to him like that. They were friends, but not close friends. And yet it was easier to talk to Alec about what was going through her head than to Bea, or Katie, or Nonna.

"Here we go..." Alec's smooth American accent drifted over from the house side of the courtyard as he placed a large jug of iced lemon water down in the middle of the table.

Rose creakily stood up and braced her hands on the small of her back. The stress of the day was seeping into her bones and, as much as she wanted to catch up with Katie, she was now wondering whether they should have carried on driving so she could have simply gone straight home and crawled into bed.

Slowly, though, as she rehydrated and nibbled on dark green olives fresh from the deli around the corner, she began to feel a little more human. And by the time the sun set, and Katie suggested a game of cards, Rose found herself saying yes.

The three of them played rummy until close to midnight, when Alec finally yawned and admitted defeat.

"I'm sorry ladies, I must still be fighting a bit of jet-lag because I'm *beat*."

"You've been in Italy for two weeks. Are you sure it's not just because we're *beating* you at cards?" Katie quipped, looking at Alec over the rim of her wine glass.

"I'm a big enough guy to admit when I've lost," Alec assured her, setting down his cards in the middle of the table. "I'll be needing a rematch sometime soon, though."

"I'll hold you to that," Katie replied, fanning out her own cards to reveal yet another winning hand.

With a roll of his eyes, Alec waved at them. "Ladies, good night."

"Good night, Alec," Rose replied. "And thank you for today."

"It was my pleasure. See you gals tomorrow."

After Alec disappeared inside, Katie and Rose sat in silence for a few long moments, drinking in one another's company and the sultry night air.

Katie was the first to speak. "So," she said, topping up Rose's glass and pushing it towards her, "what did Thomas say?"

Rose laughed, trying to deflect the question. "Have you been dying to ask that ever since I arrived?"

Katie widened her eyes, unwilling to allow Rose to change the subject.

"I don't want to put you in the middle of it," Rose said.

"You're not." Katie took a sip of wine. "You're not asking me to get involved, you're just... processing."

Rose smiled dolefully. "Well, first of all he thought I was asking for a divorce."

"Oh, blimey." Katie raised her eyebrows.

"And he said he loved me and didn't want one." Rose tapped her fingers on the side of her glass and looked down into it. "But then, when I told him we needed to sell the ranch, he said he'd rather get a divorce than sell up."

"He said that?"

"Not exactly, but it was what he meant."

Katie exhaled and shook her head.

"He doesn't want to sell. Even when he reads the details of Alec's proposal, and all the information I left behind, I'm worried he'll be too stubborn to see that it's our only option." She shrugged and pictured Thomas' face as he leafed through the paperwork. "Not that I can blame him, really. I've been thinking about this for months. He's got to get his head around it a lot quicker than that."

"You're really sure that it's the only thing left to do?" Even as Katie asked, Rose could tell that she knew the answer.

"I'm sure."

Katie pursed her lips and began to fiddle with the silver bracelet she always wore on her left wrist. "Then he'll say yes," she said confidently. "He's made mistakes. But he'll see that it's the only option. He has to, Rose."

"You think so?"

"My brother can be a pig-headed clot at times, but he knows that he's got to do something to fix what he broke. And this is the first step, isn't it?"

Rose bit her lower lip. "Katie, even if he does agree to sell, you understand that I still don't know if I can take him back."

Momentarily, the air shifted between them and became something a fraction colder. As much as Katie tried to remain neutral, she still clearly believed that if Thomas apologised and took steps to make things better, then everything could return to normal. But Rose wasn't sure she remembered how to do 'normal' anymore.

"That's your call, Rose."

"I know." Rose tried to laugh. "If only I could create a

spreadsheet or a couple of nice graphs that would tell me what to do."

After a pause, in which she looked up at the stars shimmering above the courtyard, Katie said tentatively, "What about marriage counselling? I know Thomas has been going to Gamblers' Anonymous but something for the both of you might–"

"He has?" Rose felt herself sit up a little straighter in her chair; she never thought Thomas would attend a group like that. She figured he'd be resigned to do things alone, like always.

"And physio, twice a week."

Rose lifted her glass to her lips and took a large sip. When she looked back at her friend, she said, "I know what you're doing, Katie, and I appreciate it. I know the trained psychiatrist in you must be dying to get us on a couch opening up about our feelings."

Katie laughed in agreement. "I just think it might help, that's all. Neither of you have really properly addressed the accident or what happened after. And Thomas leaving... it's a huge thing." Then she met Rose's eyes and added, solemnly, "But it's not an insurmountable thing if you still love each other."

For a moment, Rose thought Katie was about to ask whether she did still love Thomas or whether – after everything – her love for him had faded. But thankfully, she didn't. "I'll talk to Thomas. I will," Rose promised. "But right now, I need to figure out what's happening with the ranch before I can even contemplate thinking about our relationship."

"Understood." Katie smiled softly. "Understood."

21

AMELIE

"I DON'T KNOW, Cat. I just feel like something's going on."
Amelie and Cat were out by the pool. After a delicious dinner
cooked by Nonna, and a fearsome game of Monopoly, the
girls had headed outside to let the twins catch up. Skye had
eaten with them but decided not to stay for games. Despite
her disappointment, Amelie had hoped that some time as just
the four of them would encourage Ben and Ethan to snap out
of whatever was still niggling away between them.

It hadn't, though, and when Ben won, Ethan threw his
fake money on the floor and stomped out. He came back but
remained sulky and silent until Amelie announced that she
and Cat were going outside for 'girl talk' and that he and Ben
should try engaging in 'boy talk'.

"Fix whatever this is," she'd said, waving her hand at
them and channelling their mother's best and most stern
expression. "And don't come find us until you have."

Now, wondering whether the twins were finally having a

heart-to-heart with one another, Amelie was sitting on the edge of one of the loungers, holding her wine glass. She hadn't drunk from it for at least five minutes; after one too many glasses, her head felt unpleasantly fuzzy.

"Going on?" Cat slowly sipped her drink and crossed her legs at the ankles, stretching out on the sun lounger as if it was the middle of the day and not close to midnight. "With the twins? Well, yeah, obviously."

Amelie tutted. "No, Cat. Not with the twins. With Mum and Alec. Alec has been following Mum around ever since he arrived, and now they've gone on an overnight trip together?"

"They're stopping over at Aunt Katie's. Hardly a clandestine getaway. He had work to do. And Mum wanted shoes." Cat yawned, already acting bored by the conversation.

"Oh, come on. You bought that?"

"Why would they lie?"

"I keep catching them talking," Amelie said, willing Cat to see what she saw when she looked at Alec and her mother together. "And when they notice me, they stop." She waved her hands then – as its contents sloshed over the sides – put her wine glass down on the floor. "Trust me, Cat, there's something they're not telling us."

Cat sat up and tilted her head to the side, exposing a pair of cobalt blue earrings that were undoubtedly another *I'm sorry* gift from Filippo. "Okay. But even if there is something going on, so what?"

Amelie blinked hard. "*So what?*"

Cat shrugged. "Dad left home six months ago. How long is Mum supposed to sit here and wait for him to come back?"

She looked down at her nearly empty glass and then back at Amelie. "I love Dad. But he left. And Alec is nice. So, if he makes Mum happy, what's the big deal?"

Amelie felt her mouth drop open; she couldn't believe that Cat was serious. "But Mum wouldn't stop loving Dad just like that. Not overnight."

"Maybe not, but sometimes life is more complicated than that, Amelie. Not everything is black and white." Cat looked at her purposefully. "You should know that."

Amelie swallowed hard. She did know. They both did. Cat and Amelie had experienced torrid beginnings in their lives. But this was different; this was their parents they were talking about.

"Besides, are you sure you're not just projecting your own situation onto Mum and Alec?" Cat was observing her carefully.

Amelie bristled. "What do you mean?"

Cat inched forward and swung her legs around so that she was facing her sister. "You and Skye? You seem awfully close lately. *So...*" Cat drew out the word 'so' in a way that implied Amelie should be able to fill in the rest of the sentence for herself. When she didn't, Cat continued, "So, perhaps you're feeling guilty for having doubts about the wedding and you're channelling that energy into worrying about whatever is – or isn't – going on with Mum and Alec."

Amelie stood up quickly, as if the seat beneath her had suddenly caught fire. "That's utterly ridiculous! Why would I be having doubts? Skye and I are just friends, and I love Jed. I can't wait to marry him."

Cat folded her arms and stood up too. "Are you sure? Because Amelie, if you *are* having doubts – it's okay."

Amelie's skin prickled. A hot, violent shudder crept up her arms, and she looked away from her sister. When she turned back, her cheeks were flushed – and it wasn't because of the alcohol. "Cat, why would you say that?"

Cat smiled at her – a thin, sympathetic smile. Gently, she took Amelie's hand. "Because I'm your big sister and I want you to be happy." She released a small sigh. "Of all people, I know what it's like to get carried away by a situation and to feel you can't get out of it. But there's always a way out. If you're not sure that Jed is the one for you–"

Before she could stop it, fiery indignation surged up into her throat and Amelie found herself almost yelling. "Oh, right? Well, now who's projecting?!"

Cat let go of Amelie's hand.

"Just because you're stuck in a *terrible* relationship with some jerk who doesn't even value you enough to be your plus one at your sister's wedding – don't take it out on me. I love Jed. We might have only known each other a short time, but we have something *real*." Amelie stopped. She knew she was going too far. A voice in the back of her head was telling her to shut up and sit back down and apologise, but she didn't listen to it. Instead, in a low, angry voice she said, "So, perhaps, Catherine, before you wade in on my marriage and write off our parents', you should think about why you're so bitter and twisted. Your birth parents abandoned you. I get it. Mine did too. But that doesn't mean you have to tear apart every flicker of happiness that appears on the horizon."

Cat was trembling. Amelie could see it, and she was too.

She thought her sister was about to walk away, but the same stubbornness that ran through Amelie's veins ran through Cat's. So, instead, she shouted back. "I don't know why I bother. I was trying to *help* you. I was trying to tell you it's all right for you to change your mind because I love you and I care about you. But you're so wrapped up in this childish desperation to be like Mum and Dad – a whirlwind romance and then happy ever after – that you can't see what's in front of your own face." Cat was crying now but didn't wipe the tears from her cheeks. "Dad left. Mum's moving on. There are no fairy tales, Amelie. And if there are, they certainly don't involve stuck up, self-absorbed bank managers called *Jed*!"

While Cat was speaking, from the corner of her eye, Amelie registered the still blue water of the swimming pool. As anger, hurt, and guilt bubbled up in her chest, her arms suddenly shot forward. She grabbed hold of Cat's elbows and pushed, but Cat grabbed her back. And before they could stop themselves, they were tumbling into the cool dark water.

22

AMELIE

FOR A FEW SECONDS, as they looked at one another with mascara running down their faces, bedraggled hair, and sopping wet clothes, Amelie thought that she and Cat might start laughing. But then they heard Ben yelling, "What happened?! We could hear you guys shouting from up at the house..."

And the moment disappeared.

"She's impossible to speak to, that's what happened," Cat said bitterly as she waded towards the steps.

"And *she's* determined to wreck everyone else's happiness," Amelie bit back, heading for the opposite side and allowing Ben to help her out of the pool.

Wide eyed, Ben stood between them with his arms raised as if he was worried that he'd have to stop a physical fight.

"I'm going home." Cat was heading for the house. "I'll take the truck."

Quickly, Ben jogged after her. "Cat – don't be stupid, you

can't drive. You've been drinking. Come inside and get cleaned up." Briefly, he looked back at Amelie, but she turned away and wrapped her arms around herself. She was on the verge of crying and didn't want her brother to see.

As their voices faded into the distance, she began to shiver.

"Amelie?" Skye's voice made her turn around, and she smiled weakly as he laughed at her. "What on earth happened? I heard yelling..."

"Cat and I got into a fight," she said sheepishly, already feeling sorry for the awful things she'd said.

"A physical fight?" Skye looked from Amelie to the pool then, with his eyes, traced the trail of wet footprints that led away from the loungers.

Amelie shivered again. Her teeth were chattering. "First yelling and then... pushing."

Skye visibly bit back a smile and nodded slowly. "Okay. Well, you'll freeze if you don't get inside and get warm. Let's go up to the house."

Quickly, Amelie shook her head at him. "Cat's up there with Ben and Ethan, and I can't..." She paused and laced her fingers together, squeezing tightly so that her knuckles whitened with the pressure. "I need some time out before I–"

"Sure. I get it. So, come back to the cabin? You can shower and borrow some clothes."

Amelie hesitated. She should run after her sister and clear the air. But her pride wasn't quite ready to buckle. So, instead, she smiled and said, "Okay."

Back at his cabin, Skye fished a pair of joggers and a

hoodie from his wardrobe. "There are fresh towels in the bathroom. Shall I make coffee?"

"Sure. Thank you." Amelie headed for the shower and closed her eyes as the warm water washed over her, trying not to let the things she'd said to her sister spin round and round in her head.

When she emerged, no longer smelling of chlorine, and wearing Skye's clothes, he was standing in the small kitchenette pushing the plunger on a coffee pot. "Here…" He offered her a cup before filling it and adding milk and sugar.

Amelie breathed in the smell and allowed it to clear her head, although the cool water and the even cooler night-time air had done a pretty good job of that already. Leaning back on the countertop, she wrapped her fingers around the cup. "It was my fault," she said glumly.

Skye sat down in a high-backed armchair beside the unlit fireplace and tilted his head at her. "Really?"

Amelie grimaced. "Really. Cat was just looking out for me. Trying to tell me…" She trailed off, then restarted on a different tack. "She hit a nerve, and I got mad. I said things I shouldn't have – horrible things." Shame flushed her cheeks and Amelie bit her lower lip to stop herself from crying.

"I don't think I've ever seen you mad," Skye replied, perplexed. "What did she say to you?" When Amelie didn't answer, he added, "Sorry. You don't have to tell me that."

"No," she said, quickly. "It's okay. I'm just… embarrassed, I guess." Leaving her position in front of the counter, Amelie walked over to the small living space and sat down on the edge of the sofa. "She asked me if I was sure about getting married or if I was having second thoughts." Amelie had been holding her breath and tried to release it. "She thinks the only reason I'm going through with it is because I'm trying to recreate our parents' relationship. Because I believe in fairy tales..."

Skye smiled at that – a smile that made his eyes crinkle warmly as he looked at her. "There's nothing wrong with believing in fairy tales."

"Maybe not. But I think there's something wrong if you're trying to *create* one." Amelie smiled back, then ran her fingers through her damp hair. Shaking her head, she let out a hollow laugh. "I don't know. I don't think I know anything anymore."

Opposite her, Skye was silent. He took a long sip of coffee. "*Are* you having doubts?"

The question – on his lips – made Amelie blink. And instead of feeling angry, like she had when Cat asked her, she felt... nervous. "Yes," she mumbled, looking away before her eyes could betray the fizzing in her stomach. "I think I am."

After a long pause, in which both of them concentrated on the contents of their mugs instead of each other, Skye said gently, "You and Jed haven't seen one another for a while. I'm sure as soon as he arrives, things will feel... better."

But Amelie stood up and braced her hands behind her head, jutting out her elbows. "That's just it." Her damp hair tickled her cheeks as she looked up at the ceiling. "I don't think they will." She began to pace up and down, then stopped, rubbed her face with her hands and let out a low-pitched groan.

"Amelie, you can talk to me."

Amelie sat back down and leaned forward, resting her

elbows on her knees. She wanted to talk to Skye. She wanted to finally say out loud what had been bothering her for weeks. But somehow, saying it to *him* felt like even more of a betrayal towards Jed. Closing her eyes, she forced the words out.

"The way I'm feeling – it started before I left London." She hesitated, then continued. "Jed and I have only been seeing each other for a year. When he proposed, we'd been dating for six months. It was fast. But I said yes because it was all so exciting and because we seemed right for each other."

Skye nodded and waited for her to continue. His expression was neutral, perhaps too neutral, as if he was trying hard not to show any emotion at all in response to what she was saying.

"We even decided to start trying for a baby straight after the wedding..."

Skye swallowed forcefully. His lips were pressed together, but he attempted to smile at her. "If you love each other, it doesn't matter that you haven't been together very long."

"It's not just that," Amelie sighed. "After we'd decided to start a family, he suggested I quit my job."

"Your job?" Skye's forehead crinkled a little. "I thought you loved your job?"

"I do. I mean, I did. But I've always wanted to write, too. And Jed thought that if I just went ahead and stopped work, I could write my novel, take care of myself, stay home with the baby..."

Skye's eyes had widened ever-so-slightly, but he remained quiet.

"So, I did." Amelie laughed a hollow laugh. "I did it. I quit my job. I was nervous about it. Totally unsure if I was doing the right thing, but I kept telling myself that it was what we both wanted."

"Well, if it's what you both wanted–"

"But then the night before I left, suddenly, what had been a plan, set in stone, already decided... it changed."

Skye set down his mug and leaned forward too, mirroring Amelie's posture by resting his forearms on his thighs.

"He changed his mind," she said bluntly. "*Now*, Jed is saying that he's not sure when he wants children. That it's something we can discuss *after* the wedding. I thought maybe it was just a blip, but I've brought it up a couple of times on the phone and..." She lowered her head. "He simply refuses to talk about it. Or about buying a house. And now I'm wondering if those things should even be so important in the first place? If I love him, the way you're supposed to love someone when you get married, then why does it matter whether we have a baby now or next month or next year? Shouldn't I just be happy to be marrying him?" She was watching Skye as if he might truly have an answer for her.

Skye sat back and released a long, low whistle. "Have you spoken to Cat or your mum about this?"

"No. They've no idea that I left my job. Or that I'm..." She trailed off because she didn't know how to describe what she was feeling.

"Freaking out again?" Skye was trying to make her smile. But it didn't work. This time, before she could stop it, everything came tumbling out. As Skye sat and listened, Amelie told him how she and Jed had met, how perfect he'd seemed, how great everything had been.

"Planning the wedding? I rushed it. It was my idea. I was so upset about Dad leaving, and it seemed like something positive. Something I could cling on to, I guess. But the closer we get to the wedding, the more I feel like Jed's changing. And like I've changed too. Unless..." she said slowly.

"Unless?" Skye's eyes were searching hers.

"Unless we were never right for each other in the beginning."

"Do you think that's what it is?"

"I don't know. What if Cat's right? What if I was just so desperate for a fairy tale that I made it all up?"

Skye waited just half a beat before moving across to the sofa and taking Amelie's hand in his. Reaching up to stroke her hair from her face, he said, "Hey, it's going to be okay. It's all going to be okay."

Looking at him, unable to shake the confusion that was gripping her chest, Amelie leaned her forehead into Skye's shoulder and started to cry. To begin with, Skye sat stiffly beside her, unmoving. But then he wrapped his arms around her, pulled her close, and just waited until she was ready to stop.

As she pulled away, sniffing and with red puffy cheeks, he smiled at her. "Feel better?"

Amelie nodded and wiped her eyes. "A little."

"Sometimes, it's good to talk," Skye said. "Even if the person you're talking to doesn't have any answers."

"I like talking to you," Amelie said softly. Her face was close to Skye's. She could feel the warmth of his skin just whispers away from hers.

"I like talking to you, too." Skye's arm was resting on the back of the sofa. Slowly, he moved his fingers to touch her shoulder. Even through the fabric of the sweater she'd borrowed from him, she felt a flicker of electricity.

Amelie closed her eyes. She leaned forward, waiting for his lips to brush hers. But then his hand was gone. He was standing up, rubbing the back of his neck and looking at her longingly from beneath his thick dark curls. Blinking hard, as if he was trying to shift whatever feeling had lodged itself in his chest, he looked at the clock above the fireplace. "It's late. I'll make up my dad's room for you. Unless you wanted to head back to the house?"

"No," Amelie said, suddenly far too aware of the fact that the clothes she was wearing carried the lingering scent of Skye's aftershave. "I'll stay. Thank you."

"Okay then."

For a moment, Amelie thought that he might stride over and kiss her. But even as she imagined it, she knew he wouldn't; she was engaged to another man. And Skye would never, ever cross that line.

23

ROSE

W<small>HEN</small> R<small>OSE</small> <small>WOKE</small>, Katie had prepared coffee and pastries and set them out in the courtyard.

Alec was already outside and raised his coffee cup at her as she blinked sleepily at the sky.

"You look like an advert from one of those fancy over-60s holiday magazines," Rose said, taking in Alec's crisp open-necked shirt, tanned complexion, and chiselled looks. Beside him, Katie giggled, and Rose added, "Don't you think, Katie?"

Ignoring Rose's far-too-obvious attempt to whip up a spark between her two friends, Katie offered Rose a coffee and suggested that the three of them go and explore the market before she and Alec headed back to the ranch. Rose adored Lucca, and the market was one of her favourites in the area, but this morning she simply wasn't feeling up to it; her head was throbbing, and she'd woken up with a tense and painful shoulder –

something that always happened when her stress levels were high.

"I might just take a swim." She gestured to the small, raised swimming pool down by the rear wall. "Try to loosen off this stiff, aching body of mine."

Beside her, Alec cleared his throat. "I wouldn't mind a trip to the market," he said tentatively.

As Rose glanced from him to Katie, she was sure she saw a flush of pink grace her friend's cheeks. "Oh, sure. Great," Katie said, getting up from the table and deliberately avoiding Rose's gaze. "I'll go grab my things."

Smiling broadly, Alec told her to take her time; there was no rush as they weren't planning to get back on the road until after midday. Almost as soon as Katie had disappeared, he turned to Rose, opened his mouth to speak, then seemed to change his mind and close it again.

Rose fought back a smile and chewed her lower lip thoughtfully. "Everything okay?" she asked, watching Alec's expression closely.

"Oh sure, fine. Just fine," he replied.

"You know..." Rose said, not at all subtly, "Katie's an amazing woman."

Alec paused with his cup in mid-air, then lowered it back to the table and turned to look at her.

Rose raised her eyebrows, just a little, and waited for him to speak.

Finally, he said, "She is. I mean, she seems wonderful. But..." He trailed off and looked down at his wedding ring. "Is she...?"

"Oh," Rose said, realising that Katie still wore hers, too.

"No, she's not married anymore. Jerry died fifteen years ago."

"Gosh. Fifteen years." Alec exhaled slowly before meeting Rose's eyes. "I guess once you put one of these on," he said, gently turning his own wedding ring on his finger, "it's hard to contemplate taking it off. No matter the reason."

Rose smiled. Beneath the table, her hands in her lap, she touched the small but perfect diamond of her engagement ring and the band that accompanied it. "It certainly is."

24
AMELIE

"So, what's the plan today?" Skye was sitting on the short wall outside the honeymoon cabin, sipping coffee. His smile was normal. His voice was normal. But Amelie didn't feel normal.

After their almost-kiss, they had retreated to their separate rooms. She didn't know if Skye had slept, but she definitely hadn't; she'd spent most of the night staring at the ceiling and wondering how on earth she was going to get herself out of the mess she was in.

Now, stepping outside to join him, Amelie yawned, scraped her hair back, and tied it with the elastic band she'd been wearing on her wrist. Then she shimmied her arms as if she was preparing for a race. "Today, I'm going to make an apology pie and deliver it to my sister." She picked up the spare mug of coffee that was balanced beside Skye and sniffed it, allowing the scent to clear her head. Cat was her focus today. Not Jed. Not Skye. *Cat.*

"Is that a metaphor?"

"Nope. I'm making an actual pie... It's kind of a tradition. A 'Goodwin' thing." Skye was still watching her, so she explained. "Mum started it when we were kids – whenever one of us hurt a sibling's feelings, or broke someone else's toy, or borrowed their favourite dress without asking and got a giant stain on the front–"

"That seems like a very specific example," Skye cut in, chuckling at her.

Amelie nodded. "Well, that's another story. But the point is – whenever something like that happened, the person who borrowed the dress or broke the toy would make the other person an apology pie. Homemade pastry and the wronged party's favourite filling. And after that, the argument was over. No bringing it up in future fights. No grudges. A truce."

Skye smiled. "So, you're making Cat an apology pie?"

"Yep. She was trying to tell me she was there for me. And I basically threw it back in her face."

"And are you going to talk to her about..." Skye trailed off.

"My job? And the wedding?" Amelie nodded resolutely, skirting around what almost happened between them last night. "I'll try. I will."

"Good," said Skye. "Good."

Two hours later, Amelie was in the ranch kitchen wiping flour dust from her hands when Ethan sauntered in and sat down at the table. With an exaggerated yawn, he brushed his floppy hair out of his blue-grey eyes and looked pointedly at the coffee pot.

Amelie folded her arms at him. "Get it yourself," she said curtly.

"Oh, come on, I had a late night." He raised his eyebrows and wiggled them. "I was up till the early hours consoling Cat."

Giving in, Amelie poured them each a coffee and sat down opposite her brother. After brushing a wisp of hair from her face, she grimaced. "Was she upset?"

For a moment, she thought Ethan was going to deliberately try to make her feel guilty. But the flash of impishness that crossed his face soon faded, and instead he smiled thinly at her. "Nah. She'll get over it."

"I made pie," Amelie said, a little weakly.

"There you go then – she *has* to forgive you."

Amelie hung her head and looked into her coffee cup. She wasn't even particularly thirsty for it, she just wanted something to hold.

"Seriously, Am. It'll be okay. You guys have argued before. You always get over it."

"I know, but this was different. We both said things. Things we've never said before. And I pushed her into the pool. I mean..." Amelie looked up and realised that, instead of listening intently, Ethan was staring at his phone. Ducking to meet his eyes, she flicked his forehead with her index finger and said, "Gee, thanks for the advice, little brother."

Ethan rubbed at his head and screwed his eyes up at her. But then he looked down at his phone and sighed. Tapping the screen, he pushed it towards her. "That's Elena."

Amelie frowned. "Elena?" She'd never heard that name before.

"My girlfriend. Or at least, she *was* my girlfriend."

Lifting the phone, Amelie examined a photograph of a smiling woman with spirals of black hair, large hooped turquoise earrings, and a bright red coat. "She's beautiful."

Ethan let out a groan and buried his head in his hands. "I know," he muttered. "And clever, and funny, and utterly perfect."

Amelie stifled a laugh; she'd never seen her brother behave like this before and was torn between feeling sorry for him and savouring the moment so she could rib him for it later. "Ethan?" She pried his fingers away from his face. "What did you do?"

Sitting back in his chair, Ethan sighed and reached for his mug of lukewarm coffee. "We only met a few months ago. Back in February. But things were going well. Really well."

"Ah ha?"

"Except it turns out, she somehow got the impression that she was invited to the wedding."

"My wedding?"

Ethan rolled his eyes at her. "Yes – *your* wedding." He put his mug down and wrung his hands together. "And when I told her she wasn't... well, I think she thought it was because I didn't want her to come. I explained that it was because the guest list was already finalised, and all that nonsense, but she just got really quiet and distant, and then said she was going to spend the summer with her aunt in Maine, and..."

Amelie breathed in slowly, trying hard to be sympathetic

and patient despite the urge to tut and tell her brother to pull himself together. "Okay. Well, first of all, she could have come. You only needed to ask."

Ethan bit his lower lip. "Yeah. I know."

"So, you didn't want her to come?"

"No. I mean, yeah. I did. I just..." Ethan sighed. His face suddenly looked exactly as it had when he was ten years old and trying to hide that he was feeling overly emotional about something. "I wasn't sure what it would be like without Dad here. And with Ben and I not really on great terms, it felt too soon." He met Amelie's eyes. "Does that make *any* sense to you?"

"It does, actually."

"It does?"

"You like her. You want her to meet us when we're at our best. Not... disjointed."

Ethan's eyes widened. "Yeah. I think that's it."

"So, just tell her how you're feeling. She'll understand." Amelie smiled and nodded towards the kitchen counter. "Or failing that, mail her a pie?"

Amelie was packing her pie into a large tin provided by Nonna when Ethan – who'd been lingering so that he could catch a ride into *Sant Anna* with her – loudly cleared his throat and tipped his head towards the door.

Amelie looked up. She was holding the tin in front of her and was met by a mirror image of her sister in the same pose.

Slowly, Cat smiled. In unison, they said, "I made you a pie."

"Awesome," said Ethan, rubbing his hands together. "More to go around."

Cat and Amelie both shot him a 'be quiet' glance. Placing her dish down on the table, Cat said, "It's strawberry."

"Blueberry," Amelie replied, nodding at her own offering.

"Am, I'm so sorry–"

"No. Don't be silly. I'm the one who should be sorry. You were trying to help me, and I threw it back in your face."

"I should have kept my mouth shut. It's none of my business."

"Of course, it's your business." Amelie gestured to the table, and they sat down opposite one another. Nearby, Ethan was rifling through a drawer looking for forks. "I think the reason I reacted the way I did is that there was a lot of truth in what you said. I *do* crave a fairy tale, and maybe I've been glamorising Jed a little too much."

"And I'm the voice of doom and gloom," Cat said wryly. "Always expecting everything to go horribly wrong."

"Excellent," Ethan announced, sitting down at the head of the table. "So, you're both in the wrong, you're both sorry, and now... we can eat pie?"

"Oh no." Amelie waggled her finger at him and pulling away the pie dishes. Turning to Cat, she said, "Ethan has two pies of his own to make."

"Two?" Ethan was frowning at her.

"One for his *girlfriend*," Amelie said, deliberately emphasising the word.

At this, Cat whistled. "A girlfriend? How exciting."

"And one for Ben."

"Ben is not getting a pie from me," Ethan said moodily, scraping his fork against the surface of the table.

Reaching out to stop him, Cat ducked to meet his eyes. "Why not?"

"Because I did nothing wrong. I didn't quit my medical degree and abandon my brother."

"But you did react badly to your brother's decision, and made him feel very guilty about it," Cat nudged.

Ethan pouted a little and said nothing. But then he rolled his eyes. "Okay, fine. But one of you will have to help me because I have no idea where to even start. It's been years since..."

As Ethan stood up and opened the fridge to look for ingredients, Amelie and Cat scooped up their pies and tiptoed out into the entrance hall. They were halfway upstairs when they heard him yell, "Hey! Come back!"

Quickly, they ran to Amelie's room, shut the door, and sat down with their backs against it.

"Cheers." Cat raised her fork and clinked it against Amelie's.

"To apology pie," Amelie said.

"And to always being honest with one another," Cat replied. "Although maybe in the future, not *too* honest."

25

ROSE

As Alec's car pulled up in front of the ranch house, Rose heard the unmistakable sound of her children laughing. It was almost dark, but she could see their silhouettes on the veranda.

Skye was with them and, as Rose and Alec walked towards the house, Alec said to her, "Just like old times."

"Sort of," she said, quietly.

"Yes," he replied, putting a friendly arm around her shoulders. "Sort of."

They had barely reached the steps when Rose saw Amelie get up from her chair and hurry over to them. "Mum," she said, offering Rose a large, tight hug.

"Is everything all right?" Rose examined Amelie's face and noticed her daughter breathe in slowly, preparing herself to say something. "Amelie?"

Looking from Alec to Rose, Amelie nodded purposefully. "Yes. Everything's fine. And I just wanted to say that what's going on with you two? I thought it was strange at first. But now I get it."

At her sides, Rose clenched her fists. Did they know? Had Skye told them?

"I don't like the idea of you being with someone else. But you can't wait around for Dad forever, so if you and Alec are–"

Rose's eyes widened. At the same time, Alec said, rather awkwardly, "Oh, no, Amelie, you've got us all wrong. Your mother and I are just friends."

Amelie smiled at them. "Okay, well, just know that if you *are* more than friends…" she glanced over her shoulder towards her siblings and Skye, "we're all totally fine with it."

As Amelie rejoined the others, Rose exhaled loudly. "They've been talking about us," she said, unsure whether she felt like laughing or crying.

"I know." Alec chuckled, but then he looked at her and asked, "So, when are you going to tell them what's really going on?"

"I don't know." Rose wrapped her arms around her waist. "I really don't know."

26
AMELIE

Two Days Later

"Amelie? It's me."

Amelie pushed herself up onto her elbows and, as she put the phone on speaker, narrowed her eyes at the clock on her bedside table. "Cat? It's like five a.m. what's going on?"

"Filippo and I have had a fight. I need to stay here and sort it out. I'm so sorry. I won't be able to do the champagne thing. Can we rearrange? Tomorrow maybe?"

Amelie frowned and tried to remember what day it was and what Cat was talking about. "Champagne?" She sighed and rolled her eyes. Jed's champagne trip was today. She grimaced and pushed her hair back from her face. "I can't reschedule Cat – Jed arranged it. It takes months to get an appointment and he's had it booked since, like, April."

"Maybe Ben could…" Cat trailed off. Amelie could tell from the tone of her voice that she was worried about the two of them falling into another argument. But she also sounded unusually shaky, and Amelie was pretty certain she wouldn't pass up the chance to drink free champagne if it wasn't absolutely necessary.

"Don't worry, Cat. You're right. I'm sure Ben will come."

But as she hung up, Amelie remembered that Ben and her mother were both having to lead treks today. Jean was on leave, so Ben was taking over from him and Mum was leading one of the beginners' groups to the beach. Amelie glanced at her phone then, before she could think too much about it, she picked it back up and texted Skye.

Cat bailed on today's wedding activities. Mum and Ben out trekking. Fancy some free champagne?

Almost immediately, Skye replied, *Are you kidding? Who turns down free champagne? (Even if it does mean being woken up ridiculously early.)*

Great. It's a long drive. Need to leave at ten. Early bird catches the… fizzy alcohol.

Ah, that famous saying… Sure, I'll meet you out front after I've devoured some of Nonna's pancakes. Today is pancake day, right?

Amelie laughed and, even though Skye wasn't in the room, made a mock-surprised face. *Totally forgot about pancakes. I'll join you for breakfast. Veranda at eight thirty?*

Yep. Going back to sleep now, though. Will put phone on silent, so you don't keep bugging me.

After breakfast, Amelie and Skye bundled into the truck. In the passenger seat, Skye plugged the address of the vineyard into his phone and whistled through his teeth.

"It's three hours away," he said, slotting the phone into the holder on the dash.

"I know." Amelie was already feeling fed up at the thought of the long drive; it was hot, despite still being early in the morning, the truck had no air-conditioning, and the roads for the latter half of the journey would be small, winding, and precarious.

"Why this particular place?" Skye asked as Amelie pulled the truck onto the drive and headed out of the large wooden gates.

Trying not to roll her eyes, Amelie turned on the radio. "Jed tried some of their champagne at a New Year's Eve party once. He said it was the best he'd ever had, although technically I'm not sure it's called *champagne* if it's not from France?" She frowned, trying to remember what Jed had told her when he'd given her a half-hour lecture on the subject a few months ago.

Leaning his elbow on the car door and letting his hand dangle out of the window, Skye laughed. "Don't ask me, I know nothing about fancy wines."

"I don't even like it that much," Amelie said, switching radio stations and turning the volume down so it was easier to talk.

"You don't?" Skye laughed. "Then why in the world are we going all the way out to this place? Shouldn't you have wine that you *like* at your wedding?"

Amelie drummed her fingers on the steering wheel. "Yes.

Probably. But Jed thought he was doing something nice, and he was actually getting involved in at least one element of the planning, so I didn't feel like I could say no."

"Hmmm."

When Amelie looked at Skye, he was rubbing at the light dusting of stubble on his chin. "What does that expression mean?" she asked, examining him closely.

Skye held up his index finger and twitched it at her. "One second," he said, taking the phone out of its cradle. "Okay. Yes." He turned so that he was angled towards her and tapped the phone's screen triumphantly. "I have an idea."

"Okaay." Amelie wanted to look at him, but she was watching the road ahead. Giving him a furtive glance, she added, "Why do you sound mischievous?"

"Well, because why don't we play truants?"

Amelie frowned. "Truants?"

"Sure. Let's skip the fizzy grape juice and go here instead." Again, he tapped the phone. "*Forte di Viccio.* It's a thirty-minute drive, near the beach, and there's a market every weekday. I'd bet you a million dollars we can find a wine you like more than the fancy vineyard kind. And it'll be ten times cheaper, too."

Amelie shook her head. Her hair was loose and, as always happened in Italy, had developed a slight wave to it that bounced as she moved. "We can't," she said. "Can we?"

Skye shrugged. "It's your call, but it's near an awesome bit of beach – if I'm remembering correctly. And there will be food."

Amelie bit her lower lip. "I suppose... I mean, I guess I could order a couple of the bottles Jed wants for the speeches and find a different wine to go with the food? A cheaper wine." She tilted her head from side to side thoughtfully. "A wine I actually enjoy drinking."

With a twinkle in his eyes, Skye nodded. "You could…" he said, fighting an incorrigible smile.

"Okay. Let's do it. Redo the sat nav. We're heading for the beach."

The market Skye had directed them to was buzzing with colour, smells, and people. Stalls and pedestrians lined each side of the long, cobbled street that led towards the centre of the village and filled every alleyway in between.

With her sunglasses balanced on top of her head, Amelie shrugged her handbag onto her shoulder and turned to Skye. "Okay," she said. "Lead the way."

Side-by-side, they made their way past vendors selling clothes, fresh fruits and vegetables, fabrics, and food. More than once, Skye stopped to accept a sample of something – cheese, olives, chutneys, meat – and as Amelie watched him, she found it harder than ever to imagine him as a soldier. In uniform. Fighting.

Allowing her eyes to graze the scar on his forehead, once again she wanted to ask how it had happened – and why he had left.

"Am, you have to try this."

Before she could even look at what he was holding, Skye had popped a morsel of something chocolatey into her mouth.

"Wow," she said. "That's amazing."

"I'll get us some for the journey home."

"They'll melt before we even get back to the truck," she said, laughing.

"Oh, then I guess we better eat them now." Skye grinned and gestured for her to open the box he'd just bought. Sharing their chocolates, they continued through the market until Skye stopped and said, "Look, wine, just there."

Up ahead, under the shade of a large old oak tree whose roots were pushing up the slabs of the pavement around its base, a thin old man with a wiry moustache was offering thimble sized tastings of his wine to passers-by. He had just two types of bottles in front of him – red and white. And they had small, plain labels.

"We'll try one of each, please," Amelie said in her best Italian.

The man nodded. And after attempting to seem as if she was taking the tasting seriously, Amelie looked at Skye.

Smacking his lips together, he offered the man a thumbs up. "Very nice," he said, looking at Amelie to translate into Italian for him.

"*Molto Bella,*" she offered, smiling.

The man smiled too. "You would like to buy?"

"What do you think?" she asked Skye. "We can try more. There are a couple of other stalls up ahead."

But after visiting ten more stalls and trying reds, whites, sparkling wines, sweet wines, and a questionable rosé, when Skye asked Amelie if she had a favourite, she pulled him to one side and said, "Honestly? I can't tell the difference between one wine and the next. And I'm hot, and hungry, and would much rather be on the beach."

Skye smiled at her and chuckled – a soft, warm laugh that lit up his face. He was close to her, and as the smallest breeze drifted over them, Amelie caught the scent of his aftershave. Realising she was just standing there staring at him, her cheeks flushed pink. But Skye didn't seem to notice. "So," he said, "let's ask the guy by the tree if he'll deliver to the ranch, then head to the beach. His was cheapest, right?"

Amelie laughed. "Yes, it was."

"I mean, I know you and Jed aren't on a tight budget, but..."

"More money to spend on shoes, though, if we save on the drinks," Amelie said sarcastically.

"Right, so let's go get a good deal from *Signóre Moustache* over there. Then we'll head to the ocean."

Full of takeaway pasta that they'd bought on their way back to the truck, and still a little fizzy from the wine at the market, Amelie lay back and closed her eyes. Beside her, Skye did the same. They had secured fifty bottles of wine, which were going to be delivered to the ranch next week for just three euros a bottle, and she felt rather pleased with herself.

"What about the food?" Skye asked, lacing his fingers together behind his head.

"Oh." Amelie wrinkled her nose. "We booked a caterer months ago. I could have gone for a tasting, but Jed has a colleague who used them when she got married in Florence last year. So, we just went for what she'd had."

Skye had turned his head and was looking at her as though he couldn't understand a word she was saying. "Amelie, this is your *wedding* food. It's supposed to be the best meal of your life. You could have had anything… stone-baked pizza, cheesy fries, a great big pile of donuts. But you opted for… *whatever she had?*"

"I feel like you've thought more about the food you'd have at your wedding than about who you'd actually marry," Amelie laughed. "But I guess Jed's not a big foodie. And the food he does like is–"

"Fancy?" The word on Skye's lips, in his deep American voice, made her giggle.

"Yes. *Fancy*. If it was up to me, we'd have the kind of food Nonna makes. Just some great big sharing platters, some cheap wine, and chocolate for dessert."

"Well, at least we've got the wine covered."

"And the chocolate," she added. "The catering company are making 'white chocolate mousse with a cucumber and dill sorbet'."

As Amelie finished her sentence, Skye practically spat out the water he'd been drinking. "Dill? With chocolate?"

Amelie looked at him, tried to plaster a serious look on her face, and said, "I'm sure it'll be very enjoyable."

"Oh man…" Skye flopped back down onto the sand and put his hands over his face. "I'm kinda glad I'm not invited. I don't think even *my* stomach could handle dill ice cream."

"Sorbet," Amelie corrected, leaning over to nudge against him. "But of course, you're invited. If you want to…"

Skye's fingers twitched. Slowly, he parted them. "You'd want me there?"

Amelie pressed her lips together as her heart fluttered. "Your dad, too. If you're still planning on being around."

Turning to look up at the sky, and slipping his hands back behind his head, Skye nodded. "Our flights are the first week of September. So, sure. We'll be around."

"Okay then." Amelie tried to brighten her tone; something between them had shifted and she couldn't put her finger on what it was. "Great. I'll add you to the list."

A little while later, she was dozing, enveloped by the feel of the sand and the sound of the waves, when a short sharp shout made her bolt upright.

It was Skye. He was shouting. Not just shouting – screaming.

Next to her, he was tossing and turning, thrashing his arms wildly. Tears were streaming down his cheeks and beads of sweat had broken out on his forehead.

"Skye?" Amelie leaned over him. "Skye, it's Amelie." As she touched her fingertips to his shoulder, he reached for her, grabbed her wrist, and held onto it. Tight.

For a moment, he looked past her, despite the fact that his eyes were open. But then he blinked. He saw her face, looked down at his fingers around her wrist, and let go. He was trembling from head to foot. Hands raised in front of him, palms outstretched, he whispered, "Amelie, I'm so sorry. I didn't hurt you, did I? Did I hurt you?"

Amelie looked at her wrist. A small pink ring of finger marks encircled it. But they didn't hurt now that he'd let go. "I'm fine. But Skye, are *you* okay?"

"Just a dream." He was out of breath, horribly pale, and his skin was clammy. "A bad dream. That's all. I'm sorry if I scared you." He tried to smile. "Pretty glad we're the only ones on this beach."

Amelie smiled back and handed him his water bottle. "Here, drink this, and let's get out of the sun."

In the shade of the rocks, Skye sat cross-legged and drank down the entire bottle of water. In front of them, the sea was a calm and dazzling blue with pale sand stretching up and down the beach. But Skye looked as though he was seeing something completely different. "I'm sorry," he said thinly. "It's never happened in the day before."

"Don't be sorry. Do they happen a lot? Bad dreams?"

Skye met her eyes, but then looked down at his hands. "Most nights."

"And they're..?"

He inhaled sharply and touched his index finger to the scar on his forehead.

"Before you left the Army?"

Holding the now-empty bottle and picking at its label, Skye dipped his head.

"You don't have to talk about it." Amelie put her hand on his knee and ducked so she could look into his eyes "But a wise man once told me that, sometimes, it's good to talk. Even if the person you're talking to doesn't have any answers."

Skye smiled back and put his hand on top of hers. It was

175

warm, and heavy, and as his fingertips moved ever so slightly across her knuckles, her skin prickled. "I want to... with you. Just maybe not yet? Talking about my mum is different. Those are happy memories. They make me feel calm. But this stuff..."

Amelie tried to nod, but she was staring at their hands. She swallowed hard and when she looked up, Skye was watching her.

As if in slow motion, he gently took his hand back and brushed his fingers through his curly hair.

Amelie's cheeks felt hot, and she wasn't sure if it was from the sun or from the heat of Skye's gaze. For a while, they sat together and watched the waves lap the shore. Then, standing and brushing sand from her shorts, Amelie waved her arms towards the road. "We should probably get going."

Skye stood up too and put his hands into his pockets. "Yeah," he said. "I guess we should."

27

ROSE

Rose was out back with Ben and Ethan, drinking wine by the fire pit and breathing in the scent of Nonna's oregano, when she finally heard the truck pull in through the front gates.

"They've been gone hours," Ethan said pointedly.

Pretending she didn't notice her son's tone of voice, Rose moved her glass over a small water stain on the table and replied, "Well, it was a long journey. A three-hour drive, at least."

"Mum?" Amelie's voice filtered through from the entrance hall.

"Out here," Rose called. "With your brothers."

Emerging from the kitchen, Amelie smiled widely at them. She looked bouncy and happy, and Rose hoped she hadn't sampled too much wine at the vineyard before driving back.

"So, how was it?" she asked. "Did you taste the world's *best* champagne?"

Exchanging a look with Skye, who was standing beside her, Amelie laughed a little and said, "No. We didn't. But we did get our hands on fifty dirt-cheap and very tasty bottles from the market in *Forte di Viccio*."

"And then we went to the beach," Skye finished, sitting down next to Ethan and patting him on the shoulder in greeting.

Rose frowned at Amelie. "So, you didn't go to the vineyard?"

"It was miles away and I don't even like champagne. So, I made an executive decision to change plans."

"Which beach?" Ben asked.

"That little deserted cove near the town," Amelie said. Then she turned to Skye. "I'm going to make tea. Do you want one?"

"Sure, I'll give you a hand."

Skye and Amelie were in the kitchen, searching for the stash of Nonna's special nutmeg tea, when Rose heard her daughter say loudly, "Cat? What's happened?"

Moments later, Amelie appeared with her arm around her sister's waist.

Cat – who usually looked like a supermodel, with her shoulder length dark hair, immaculate clothes, and brightly coloured accessories – was wearing a grey jersey lounge suit and had clearly been crying.

"She broke up with Filippo," Amelie said sympathetically, shooting the boys a look that told them to keep any sarcastic comments to themselves.

"Oh, sweetheart." Rose pulled Cat onto her lap as if she was still a tiny child and kissed her cheek. "Go make her some tea, Amelie, and put plenty of sugar in it."

"Already done." Skye had walked outside holding a tray of mugs and set it down on the table.

Looking up and sniffing, Cat slid into her own chair and took one. "Thank you."

"What happened?" Amelie put a hand on her sister's shoulder.

"Oh," Cat said sharply, "you know. Same as usual. He's a jerk. I tried to get him not to be. He said I was too high maintenance. We argued. And then he..." She gulped down a large swig of tea, even though it was still far too hot to drink. "And then he broke up with me."

"Sorry, Cat." Ben reached out to pat her hand and offered her a sympathetic smile.

"Yeah," Ethan chimed in, "sorry. Although, to be fair, he sounds like an idiot. You're better off–"

Rose shook her head at him.

"Too soon?" Ethan wrinkled his nose in agreement. "Yeah, too soon, sorry."

After dissecting her and Filippo's argument for another half hour or so, finally, Cat seemed a little brighter. "Well," she said, forcing a smile to her lips and looking at Rose. "At least I don't have to work in that silly gelato store anymore. You need a new receptionist; I'll just work here for a while."

Noticing the unflinching look on Rose's face, she added, "Don't worry, Mum, I'm super cheap."

Rose smiled thinly and gripped the handle of her mug. "I'm sure you are, darling, but…"

"Ooh," Amelie said excitedly, "does this mean you're moving back into the ranch house?"

"I guess so." Cat shrugged. "I have nowhere else to go. That's okay, right, Mum?"

"Of course, it is." Ben answered before Rose had the chance to. He was smiling. "*Heart of the Hills* will always be home, that's what you said when I moved back, right Mum?"

"We are so lucky." Cat was pouring herself a drink, and the children were slipping into a sweet, nostalgic conversation that made Rose's heart hurt.

After a few minutes, she couldn't listen to it anymore. "I'm sorry," she said loudly, watching them all stop and look at her. "I have something to tell you. I should have told you sooner, but I was waiting for the right time. And I know now that there won't be a right time, so I just need to…"

Around the table, Amelie, Cat, Ethan, and Ben were staring at her as if they were terrified of whatever she was about to say. But Skye had a different look on his face; he knew what she was going to tell them. And Rose suddenly felt horribly guilty that he was going to be roped into it. Offering him a thin smile that she hoped was apologetic, she cleared her throat and – so that she had something to hold – picked up her empty wine glass.

"This isn't going to be easy. I'd hoped your father would be here to talk to you about it with me. But–"

"For goodness' sake, Mum, you're scaring us," Cat said. "What is it? You're not ill, are you?"

"No. Nothing like that. I'm fine." Rose inhaled slowly then, after far too many empty seconds, said the words she'd been dreading for weeks. "But the ranch isn't."

As she explained what had been happening, detailing their father's gambling debts and how they were crippling the ranch, Rose watched each of her children's eyes gloss with tears. Cat and Ethan held them back, pursing their lips and sitting very still in their chairs. But Amelie didn't and Ben was losing his battle too.

"I'm so sorry, Mum," Amelie breathed. "I had no idea things were so bad. I should have visited more. I should have–"

Rose put down her glass. "Sweetheart, I'm afraid I'm not finished. You see, I've investigated every option. I've been over the figures again, and again, and again. But there's only one way out of the mess we're in."

Here it came… she wasn't even nearly ready. But she had no choice.

"We have to sell *Heart of the Hills*."

28

THOMAS

THOMAS POURED himself a glass of whisky and wrapped his fingers around it. He had walked for over an hour to buy it, and his hips were throbbing.

In front of him, spread out on the small fold-out table in the corner of the hut, were the papers that Rose had left him with. It was late. Just a small, muted lamp lit the room and, outside, the meadow was eerily quiet. He had read the contents of the file over and over through eyes thick with tears. Each time, a voice in his head had whispered loudly, *She's right. You know she's right. And this is all your fault.*

As he lifted the glass to his lips, he paused. It had been five months since he last had a drink. He'd arrived at the cabin as a shell of a man and had drowned himself in whisky for at least two weeks. It was something he had never done; he was the kind of guy who liked a drink at parties or on special occasions, but who could take it or leave it the rest of the time. Being drunk did not suit him.

Rossi, of all people, had been the one to remind him that replacing betting with booze was probably the worst thing he could do.

"Tom, come on now, this isn't you," he had said in his deep Italian voice, putting his hand firmly on Thomas' shoulder. And even when Thomas had tried to shrug him off, his old friend had persevered. "Give me the bottle, Tom. You came here to get yourself together. You asked to stay here so you could get yourself *together* and get your family back."

Eventually, Thomas had handed it over.

He hadn't touched a drop since. But now, thinking of a future without the ranch and without Rose, he was dangerously close to believing that the work he'd done to mend himself over the past few months had all been for nothing.

He was staring at the glass, moving it in a slow circle and watching the water ring that was forming beneath it, when the phone on the cabin wall began to ring.

He waited, hoping it would stop. But when it didn't, he forced himself to stand up and answer it.

"Hello? Rossi's cabin."

"Dad?"

Thomas' breath caught in his chest.

"Dad, it's Ethan. We need you to come home."

29

AMELIE

WHEN ETHAN HUNG up the phone, Amelie looked at her brother and said, "Ben won't be pleased."

"Neither will Mum," Ethan added.

"Did we do the right thing?"

"Do you want to lose this place?" He was looking out at the sprawling twilight hills in the distance and had shoved his hands into his pockets.

"Of course not, but if Mum says it's the only way..." Amelie was having doubts. Already, she felt horribly guilty for betraying her mother's trust. It had been an impulse. A gut reaction which told her that, despite what she now knew about the secrets he'd been hiding, there was no way her father would let this happen. There was no way he'd let them lose their home.

She had sat and listened to it all. She'd taken it in, and she'd understood it. But she still couldn't bring herself to believe that selling the ranch was the only way.

Ethan pursed his lips thoughtfully – always one to be driven more by logic than emotion. "That's not the point. The point is, we should be making this decision together. As a family. Dad needs to be part of it." Ethan looked at her pointedly. "The Andersons shouldn't be the ones driving this," he said. "It should be us. All of us. Together. Talking it through."

Amelie nodded, but deep down she was wondering whether her brother was right; should she and her siblings be a part of the decision-making process? It was their childhood home, but ultimately it was her parents' lives and livelihoods at stake.

And no matter how angry she was with Skye for keeping this huge, enormous secret from her, she didn't believe that he and Alec had taken advantage of Mum – swooped in when she was vulnerable to secure a good deal. In fact, Mum said Alec had been incredibly generous with his offer. And that *she* had been the one to reach out to him about the sale because she knew he'd always dreamed of owning a ranch someday.

"Do you think he'll come?" Amelie asked, leaning onto the railings.

"Of course, he will." Ethan was fiddling with a splinter of wood on the rail beside her. After a pause, he said, "I can't believe Skye didn't tell us. Or you, at least. You two have been glued to one another since you got here."

Swallowing hard, Amelie tried not to think about all the times that she and Skye had been together. All the times she'd been beating herself up for enjoying his company so much. All the times he'd been holding back the true reason he came to Tuscany. Not for a holiday or a change of scenery, but for a change of *life*. If the sale went ahead, Skye and Alec would be the ones living in the ranch house. Skye and Alec would be the ones who woke up every day to horses, and sunshine, and Nonna's cooking.

"I know," she muttered, pinching her teeth together to stop yet more tears from falling. "I can't believe it either."

Her first reaction when her mother told them they needed to sell had been outrage. Like her siblings, she had launched into a litany of reasons it was simply not possible for them to lose their childhood home. But then, as the others cooled down and Mum tearfully told them how truly sorry she was, Amelie had looked at Skye.

The whole time, he'd remained silent. But as their eyes met, she had literally gasped at the realisation that he'd known, all along, about the sale. And that he hadn't told her.

At that moment, instead of staying and allowing him to speak, she had stood up from the table and marched out. And now, as she fought back the swirling, nauseous feeling in her gut, she screwed her eyes shut at the thought of him.

"Still," said Ethan. "Maybe it's for the best?"

"Selling the ranch?" Amelie's mouth dropped open. "But you said–"

"No, not the ranch – Skye." There was a look on Ethan's face that Amelie didn't see very often; he was usually the joker, the sarcastic one, the blunt one. But suddenly he looked... empathetic. "You two seem close but you're getting married to someone else, Am. So, maybe it's for the best that he wasn't who you thought he was?"

Amelie nodded. Looking up at the velvet sky, the most beautiful sky she'd ever seen, she leaned her head on Ethan's shoulder. "Yes," she said. "Maybe it is."

30
ROSE

Nearly twenty-four hours after telling her children the news that she knew had broken their hearts, Rose was walking up from the stables when she stopped in the middle of the path. The empty bucket she'd been holding dropped from her hand and she braced her hands on her lower back.

"Thomas?"

Her husband's unmistakable figure had appeared near the house at the edge of the tree-lined driveway. He was waiting for her.

After taking a deep breath, Rose picked up the bucket and pressed forward. When she reached Thomas, she folded her arms in front of her and looked him up and down.

"You didn't tell me you were coming."

"I didn't know I had to."

"Well," she bit back – quicker than she'd expected – "you've been gone for quite a few months, so some notice would have been nice."

Slowly, Thomas nodded, but he didn't respond to her jibe. Instead, he presented the folder she'd left him with. "I looked through it all," he said.

Reluctantly taking it from him, Rose tried to look unflustered.

"Perhaps we should talk about this properly... inside?" Thomas looked at the house with an almost wistful expression on his face.

"Here is fine." Rose tucked the folder under her arm. "What's your decision?"

Softening a little and pulling his eyes away from the front of the ranch house, Thomas rubbed the back of his neck. "I can't sign the contract, Rose. I can't sign the ranch away."

"I should have known." Rose had spent most of the previous evening crying. She had no tears left. She was empty and exhausted, and she had no options left. "Then *you* fix it," she said, waving at their vast beautiful property. "Fix this, Thomas. Because I don't know what else to do."

"Rose..." Thomas was smiling at her. He was moving closer, as if he was about to take her in his arms and tell her everything would be okay. "I'm here now. We can figure it out. We can–"

"Don't." She snapped her arm away from him. "Just... don't."

31

THOMAS

"ROSE, PLEASE." Thomas jogged awkwardly after his wife and tried to take hold of her elbow. Again, she pulled away from him, so he stepped in line beside her and said, "Okay, listen, I should have told you about the money. Heck, I shouldn't have gotten into that mess in the first place. And I definitely shouldn't have run away from it. But this isn't the way to handle it. You can't sweep away our entire life's work and ruin our marriage just to punish me. I wasn't unfaithful Rose. I didn't have an affair or murder someone. It's just money. Money… that's all."

Rose stopped. She was facing the ranch house and Thomas could see her shoulders trembling as they moved up and down in time with her breath. Finally, she spun around to face him.

Thomas swallowed hard; he'd rarely seen her angry but, in that second, her features shimmered with fury.

"You really don't get it, do you?" she asked.

Thomas tried to reply, but she cut him off.

"I couldn't give a jot about the money, Thomas. I could even forgive the lying."

For a moment, a brief glorious moment, Thomas' heart felt lighter. Until he realised that she wasn't finished.

"But this isn't *my* doing. *I'm* not the one ruining our marriage because what I can't forget – the thing that shakes me to the core whenever I think about it, the thing which broke me into a million pieces that I've been clamouring to find and put back together – is that you *left* me."

When she stopped, Rose let her words hang in the air and just stared at him.

"We came up against the first real trauma of our married lives and, two days after our twenty-ninth anniversary, you quit. You walked out. You didn't think about me, or what it would mean for me, or how I'd cope. You might not have had an affair. But you left." Her voice faltered and she put her hand on her chest, searching his face with watery eyes. "You *left*."

Rose's fury had turned to sorrow, and Thomas could barely look at it. Etched all over her beautiful face – a face he'd loved for what felt like his entire life – was the kind of hurt he'd never seen in her before and had never wanted to see.

Rose gently wiped her eyes. Her shoulders drooped, as though the strength she'd been holding on to since his accident had suddenly evaporated.

"Rose..."

She waved a hand at him and looked back at the house. Her hair was loose, threads of silver glistening as the sunlight touched them. "I'm not saying there isn't a way back," she said quietly. "But I can't undo the way I feel just by deciding I don't want to feel it anymore." She met his gaze and held it. "And whatever we do with the ranch, Thomas, is a separate decision. It's not about us. It's about the business."

"I understand," he said.

And he did. He finally understood.

32
AMELIE

Three Days Later

"WHAT TIME IS HE ARRIVING, DARLING?"

Amelie was fidgeting with a vase of flowers on the kitchen table while her mother – who looked as if she hadn't slept properly for days – frantically finished sweeping the floor.

"This afternoon but..." Amelie put her hand on her mother's arm, "Jed's not the King of England. There's no need to stand on ceremony."

Smiling but still gripping the handle of the broom rather tightly, Mum breathed out slowly. She was wearing cut-off jeans and a long loose shirt, and she looked beautiful even though she'd been cleaning all morning. "I know, but I want to make a good first impression. I still can't quite believe that you're getting married in under a week and I haven't met him yet. It was all so fast, wasn't it?"

Amelie leaned back on the edge of the table. "I know, I'm sorry. We should have tried to get out here sooner. His job is just so–"

Mum waved a hand at her as if it wasn't a big deal. "Full on. Like yours."

"Yes." Amelie was fiddling with the hem of her pale blue top and was glad that her mother didn't turn around to notice the guilt that was written all over her face. She still hadn't told her family about leaving her job. She hadn't even told Cat, despite promising Skye that she'd try to after their argument by the pool.

As her thoughts flitted towards Skye, she flexed her fingers and tried not to wonder what he'd been doing since they last spoke. The day after Mum told them what had been going on, not long after sunrise, he had sought Amelie out and had apologised. Walking slowly around the neat Italian gardens by the pool, he explained that Alec had told him about wanting to buy the ranch on their very first night at *Heart of the Hills*.

"Dad asked what I thought about it – if it was something I'd like to be a part of. And honestly? I said yes. Of course, I'd be a part of it. After everything that's happened over the past few years, I couldn't think of anything better than being here. *Living* here. Having something new to focus on."

"I get that," Amelie had said, sitting down on the cool stone bench beside the rose bushes and looking up at him. "But why didn't you say anything? All this time..."

Hesitantly, Skye had sat down next to her. "Dad asked me not to. He said that your mum was having a really tough time with the decision."

"I see."

With a sharp intake of breath, Skye had added, "But I didn't know about the gambling. Not until last night."

At first, as Amelie listened to him, anger had quivered on the tip of her tongue. But when she looked at his face and saw the dejection swimming in his eyes, the feeling subsided.

"I'm not mad," she said, eventually. "But I am confused, and hurt, and there's too much going on in my head for me to decide whether I can go right back to being friends."

"I understand."

Nodding, Amelie had stood up and walked away. But before she'd reached the arch in the hedge that led back towards the house, she had turned back to him. "Thank you for apologising."

"Thank you for listening." Skye had stood up to watch her leave.

"I'll talk to you soon," she'd promised.

But it had been three days since they last spoke. Three days in which Skye had avoided her and she had avoided him.

She was about to ask Mum if she knew where he was, because the silence between them was slowly and silently killing her, when her mother triumphantly put down the dishcloth she'd been holding. "There. Done." Turning to put on the kettle, she added, "But you're sure Jed won't mind staying in one of the normal cabins? Skye and Alec said they'd be happy to swap. And I can ask housekeeping to..."

Amelie snapped out of her Skye-scape and took two clear glass mugs out of the cupboard beside the sink. "He won't mind," she said, even though she was sure that Jed probably *would* mind.

"Good. And does he know yet?"

Amelie frowned as she took two sachets of green tea from a packet and placed them delicately into the glass mugs.

"That you're no longer following the wedding diet?" Her mother's eyes sparkled as she spoke, and it made Amelie smile.

The pair of them were laughing and heading towards the shaded table outside the kitchen doors when Amelie's phone rang. "It's Jed," she said with a twinge of nervousness in her voice. Then, pressing the green 'answer' button, "Hi. Your flight isn't delayed is it? Ben will be leaving any minute now to pick you up."

On the other end of the phone, she could hear Jed's voice, but it was muffled, and he clearly wasn't speaking to her as he said, "Yeah, one minute. She'll be fine with it."

"Jed? Hello?"

"Amelie. There you are. It's great to hear your voice."

"Yours too. I feel like we've barely spoken since I left."

"I know. I know." There was a drawl in Jed's tone that Amelie hadn't noticed before, and it made her skin feel strangely uncomfortable. "But listen, babe, I'm just about to get on the plane and I've been talking to the guys – we were thinking we might stay in Pisa for a few days before heading to the ranch. See the leaning tower and all that. Seems a shame to miss it when we're here."

Amelie swallowed hard and glanced at her mother, who was sipping her tea and clearly trying not to look as if she was listening to their conversation. "The *guys*?" As far as

Amelie knew, Jed was travelling out alone, and the rest of the guests were flying in the day before the ceremony.

"Ah. Didn't you get my email?"

There had been no email. Amelie was sure of it.

Lowering his voice, Jed said quickly, "I didn't think there was any harm in it. It's just me, Hugh, Eddie, and Pete. That's all."

Amelie pursed her lips and inhaled deeply through her nostrils. She knew they would be twitching and could feel her cheeks growing hot as she bit down on what she really wanted to say. Hugh, Eddie, and Pete were Jed's designated groomsmen. But they were also clients. Important clients. And this was clearly his way of impressing them. "Fine," she said bluntly. What else was there to say?

"Am, come on. Don't be like that. It's only a couple of days. I'll still be there in plenty of time to help out with–"

"No, you won't. But it's fine, Jed. I'll see you in a few days. Let me know, though, won't you, when you're planning to arrive? Mum's been working her socks off all morning, so it would have been nice to have more than a few hours' notice that you're not bothering to turn up." As she finished speaking, she held her breath. But before Jed could reply, she hung up and, squeezing the phone tightly in her fist, let out a low, frustrated growl.

Mum put down her tea. "He's not arriving today?"

Amelie expected to feel tearful, but the only sensation coursing through her veins was a mixture of annoyance and disbelief. "No. He's staying in Pisa to see the tower. With some friends from work."

Mum opened her mouth as if she was trying to think of

something to say that would excuse Jed's behaviour but, unable to think of anything, closed it again and smiled softly at Amelie. "I'm sorry," she said. "I know you were looking forward to seeing him."

Amelie nodded but, as she did, she looked away. Because, really, she hadn't been looking forward to seeing him at all. She'd been dreading it.

Since she arrived at the ranch, she'd been telling herself that if she could just *see* Jed, then all her doubts and worries would fade away. She'd look at him and she'd remember that they were good together, and that he loved her, and that she loved him. But the closer it had gotten to the day when he was due to land in Italy, the more terrified she'd become that she would look at him and *not* see those things. It was as if being back home at the ranch had drained all the London out of her and replaced it with nothing but sunshine and horses and family. As if she was someone completely different from the woman who left England a few weeks ago.

She'd almost said as much to Cat when she apologised for their fight, and Cat had told her – just like Skye had – that everything would be okay. Probably Mum would say the same thing. But what if it wasn't okay? What would she do then?

"Listen..." Mum pulled Amelie in for a hug and squeezed her tightly. "Why don't you and Cat do something to take your mind off it? She needs a bit of TLC after her split with Filippo. Maybe take the boys too? I'm sure the four of you could use some sibling time." Her mother stood back and smiled tentatively. "The last few days have been a little... full on."

Amelie nodded. It had been full on. Since her day at the beach with Skye, events had tumbled on, one after another, at increasing speed. Life-changing events. Things she'd never expected to have to deal with. She had been furious with Mum for lying to them, furious with Skye, and even more furious with her father. But when the fury had faded, all that was left was sadness. And it was close to overwhelming her.

"Good idea," she said, not wanting her mother to see that she was still battling to seem upbeat about the prospect of selling to Alec and Skye.

"Maybe ask Skye too?" Mum blinked hesitantly. "You know, it wasn't his fault, Amelie. I asked Alec to keep it from you all until I'd settled things with your father and until the wedding was over. I didn't want to–"

"Mum, it's okay. I know." Amelie reached for her now lukewarm tea and sipped it. "I'm not angry with you. I understand why you didn't say anything and why Skye had to keep it from me. But that doesn't mean it doesn't hurt."

She had walked over to the table and pulled out a chair to sit down beneath the parasol. By the steps up into the herb garden, one of Nonna's chickens was pecking delicately at the ground. As her mother sat down opposite, Amelie sighed. Her teabag had burst, and loose tea leaves were swirling in her cup. "I thought we had... something. Me and Skye. A friendship. I thought we *got* one another." Amelie rolled her eyes at herself. "It's hard to explain. I just felt as if there was a *truth* between us. Not necessarily something we said to each other, just an understanding... but the whole time, he was keeping something from me."

"Sweetheart..." Mum reached out and took Amelie's

hands between hers. "Something I've learned over recent months is that nothing is black and white. Feelings are complicated. Circumstances are complicated. Your father lied to me but, ultimately, he did it because he was trying to protect me from the truth. Not to hurt me."

Amelie looked up. "So, you're not angry with him for lying?"

Her mother breathed in slowly, patting Amelie's hands beneath hers. "I am. But I'm also sad. And I also miss him. And I'm angrier with him for leaving than for lying."

"Do you think you'll get back together?" The question left her lips before her brain considered whether it was appropriate to ask. Her and Ethan's late-night phone call to their father had worked; Dad had turned up the next day and had been sleeping in a recently vacated cabin ever since. But with his absence at dinner and the sparse words exchanged between him and Mum when they crossed paths, it still felt as if he wasn't really there.

Mum reached up to adjust the loose bun that sat at the nape of her neck. "I'm not sure we were ever truly apart," she said pensively. "But honestly, Amelie, I don't know. For the first time in a long time, I don't know what the future holds for your father and me. And *that* is scary."

33

AMELIE

AT THEIR FAVOURITE SWIMMING SPOT – a deep pool fed by a small waterfall – Amelie and Cat watched as Ben and Ethan raced each other back and forth in the water. The girls had been swimming too but were now taking picnic food and bottles of water from their bags and setting them out on a blanket.

"Are they friends again yet?" Cat asked, gesturing to the twins.

"Nope. Not yet." Amelie waved at their brothers and called for them to come and eat.

As they stepped out of the water, Amelie smiled. "It still amazes me exactly how *the same* you guys are, even though you're not technically identical," she said, looking at their spookily similar faces.

"Not totally alike." Ethan narrowed his eyes sharply at Ben.

"Okay…" Amelie stood up and put her hands on her hips.

"That's it. You two need to figure out whatever's going on here. Because it's not right. You've never fought for this long before." She turned to Ethan. "I thought you were going to make Ben an apology pie. What happened?"

"I never agreed to that," Ethan mumbled. "And like I said, I don't think I have anything to apologise for."

"Leave it, Am," Cat said, gesturing for her to sit down. "We can't force them to get on. They'll sort it out, eventually."

Amelie was reluctant to give in. But when everyone else started eating, and ignoring her, she rolled her eyes and sat down beside Cat.

After a few awkward moments of no one speaking, Ethan finally said, "So, do you think they'll really sell the ranch?"

"Doesn't sound like they've got much choice," Cat replied.

"Surely, there must be something they can do?" Ethan was chewing and talking at the same time.

"I don't know," Amelie said, putting down her food. "Mum's pretty good at the financial side of things. I'm not sure she'd suggest selling up if it wasn't the only viable option."

"You've changed your tune. A few days ago, you were all for calling Dad and getting him back home to sort it out."

"You called Dad?" Ben asked, open-mouthed. As Amelie had predicted, he had not been happy when their father showed up at the ranch. And she hadn't dared tell him that it was her and Ethan who'd asked him to come.

"Yes," Ethan said, defiantly. "We did."

Ben's eyes narrowed, and he looked like he was about to say something, but then he simply chewed at his lower lip.

"You don't think he should be involved in what's going on?" Ethan had latched onto their difference of opinion and was using it as a chance to argue, staring at Ben and goading him into answering.

To Amelie's surprise, when Ben looked up, slowly and carefully, he said, "No. I do not. He racked up thousands in debt. He left our mother to cope with it alone. Why don't you see that he doesn't deserve to be a part of anything anymore?"

"He's still our father, you ungrateful–" Ethan stood up and marched over to Ben.

"Ungrateful?" Ben stood up too and squared up to his brother.

"Yes. Ungrateful. And speaking of money – you quit halfway through a medical degree that they'd already nearly bankrupted themselves paying for. You wasted it. Threw it down the drain. At least in a few years, I'll be on a good enough wage to help them out. Where will you be? Still scrounging off them and bumming around with the horses?"

"I quit so I could *save* them money, you idiot!" Ben's face had turned a violent shade of red. "I knew about Dad's debts. I found out the summer that *I* came home to help them. How could I go back to America and let them keep paying for me, subsidising my expensive education, when I knew how much of a mess they were in?"

Amelie heard Cat gasp.

Ethan's expression remained very, very still. And then he said, in almost a whisper, "What? You did *what*?"

Looking at Amelie and then Cat, Ben sucked in his cheeks and blinked hard. "I knew," he repeated. "So, I quit." Then to Ethan, he said, "You were always going to be a better doctor than me. My heart wasn't in it."

Ethan looked as though he couldn't take in what Ben was saying. Slowly, he stepped back and leaned against a nearby tree. "Ben…"

"Does Mum know?" Amelie asked, standing up and going to Ben's side so she could put her hand on his shoulder. "Does she know that's why you quit?"

"No." Ben looked green around the edges. "I didn't tell either of them I'd found out. If I had… if I'd spoken up, he'd have had to tell her sooner. He wouldn't have left." Ben leaned forward and braced his hands on his knees, breathing hard.

Looking sharply at Ethan, Amelie beckoned for him to come closer. At last, Ethan shook himself out of his malaise and crouched down in front of his brother.

"Hey," he said. "None of this is your fault. And… I'm sorry." He nudged Ben's arm so that he was forced to look at him. "I'm sorry I misjudged the situation." Smiling, he added, "I thought you were just a lazy swine who couldn't be bothered to work."

As Ethan spoke, Amelie held her breath. Cat was doing the same. But then Ben's shoulders shook, and he let out a loud, "Ha!"

Clapping him on the back, Ethan began to laugh too.

"What a mess," Cat said. "What a great big, ridiculous mess this family has been."

"Right," Ethan agreed. "So how are we going to fix it?"

34

ROSE

T H E   C H I L D R E N   A R R I V E D   B A C K   from the woods practically glowing. Amelie and Cat were arm-in-arm while Ben and Ethan were jostling one another as if they'd never been anything but best friends.

From the veranda, Rose watched them amble up the path towards the house and hugged her arms around her waist. Then she spotted Thomas. He had been down by the pool and must have heard the kids' voices because he emerged from behind the hedge that backed onto the sun beds and waved at them. As was customary, he was wearing a cowboy hat – the kind that Rose had always made fun of him for – and it brought a soft smile to her lips.

As she watched, however, her smile wavered.

All four children had stopped – paused as if in a freeze frame – and none of them was speaking.

For the few days that Thomas had been back, the children had stayed firmly out of his way and – despite everything –

their hesitancy made Rose's heart ache for him. *Never* would she have imagined a world in which Amelie and Catherine didn't run straight up to their father and tuck themselves under his arms. Or when Ben and Ethan wouldn't grin at him and chatter away excitedly about what they'd been up to.

Ethan was the first to break ranks. Slowly, he walked over to pat his dad on the shoulder. They spoke for a moment; the others hanging back. But then they continued on their way up to the house and Thomas stepped in line beside them.

Rose contemplated going inside and trying to avoid him, but before she could decide, they were in front of her.

"Mum, is it all right if Dad joins us for dinner?" Ethan said directly. "Ben's got something he wants to tell you both."

"I have too," Amelie said loudly from behind her brother.

Rose looked at Thomas, who shrugged to indicate that he had no idea what they were talking about. "Okay," she said tentatively. "I haven't prepared anything though. I was going to suggest that we ate out front with the guests tonight. One of the larger groups is heading off on an overnight trek with Jean. So, there'll be room."

"Ooh, good idea." Cat pushed her sunglasses onto the top of her head. "I love watching the sun set from out here. Am and I will go freshen up. See you in a bit?"

"Sure."

As she headed off with Amelie, Cat gave the boys a 'look' – clearly hinting for them to leave Rose and Thomas alone for a few minutes. Obediently, Ethan and Ben took the hint and mumbled something about wanting to hang up their swim gear and shower.

Alone, except for the guests who had already started to wander up for early takings of Nonna's food, Thomas leaned his arms on the railing in front of them and took off his hat. "Thanks. It'll be nice to eat with the kids."

"Seems like they have something they want to say." Rose turned so that her back was resting against the railings beside him. She knew she was frowning but was surprised when Thomas moved a little closer to her and said softly, without touching her, "I'm sure it's nothing to worry about. They seemed happy."

Stopping herself from sighing, Rose nodded. "They did. The happiest I've seen them in a while." As she spoke, she bit her lower lip and glanced at her husband; she wasn't deliberately trying to make him feel guilty. But it seemed like everything she said to him was laced with the implication that he had made their lives very, very difficult. He had. But it wasn't fair of her to keep reminding him of it.

"Sorry. I didn't mean to–"

Thomas shook his head. "It's okay, Rose. And listen, we should have a conversation too. About Alec, and this place, and what we're going to do. I've been doing a lot of thinking these past few days and we should talk. Properly talk."

"Tonight? After dinner?"

Thomas put his hat back on and stood up. "Tonight."

As the heat of the sun faded from the day, and most of the guests retreated to their cabins or down to the pool for an after-dinner dip, the Goodwins settled into chairs around a large oval-shaped table on the veranda. Ethan poured them each a glass of wine and Nonna brought out huge trays of whatever was leftover in the kitchen.

"Join us." Rose gestured to an empty seat. "Please?"

Looking only at Rose – she hadn't spoken to Thomas since his arrival – Nonna replied, "No. Thank you, *Cara Mia*, I will tidy the kitchen first. I must supervise the new girl at all times."

"After?"

"Perhaps," said Nonna, turning to walk back inside.

As she disappeared, and before any of them had even begun to load their plates with food, Ethan cleared his throat and tapped his plate with his knife. "Before we start, who's going first? Ben or Amelie?"

Rose put down her wine glass, folded her hands in her lap, and braced herself for whatever they were about to say.

"I'll go first." Ben nodded at his brother then, taking a deep breath and speaking more to Rose than to Thomas, he said, "I knew about Dad's debts."

Rose's skin instantly went cold.

"I was looking for some forms in the office one day and I found the paperwork. Letters from the bank. Credit card statements." Ben's face was incredibly pale and his voice a little hoarse. "I shouldn't have looked through them. I'm sorry."

"When was this?" Rose asked finally, feeling both winded and dizzy from her son's revelation.

"Last summer." Ben looked as if he might vomit.

"A year ago? You've known for a year?" Thomas was leaning forward onto his elbows, staring at Ben with an expression Rose couldn't read. She wanted to reach for his hand because she knew that he too would be feeling the weight of what Ben had been carrying around all this time.

"Yes."

"That's why he stayed here instead of going back to New York," Ethan said. "He thought that if you didn't have to worry about supporting his medical degree, it might make things easier."

Thomas sat back in his chair. He looked unsteady, as if he was on the deck of a small boat and being rocked by a storm. "Ben," he breathed, pushing his fingers through his hair and breathing out a low whistle.

Rose had been trying desperately hard not to cry, but as Ben's eyes filled with moisture so did hers. "Sweetheart, I'm so sorry."

Trying to laugh, Ben took a drink from his wine glass. "It's fine, really. I wasn't going to be much of a doctor. Couldn't stand the sight of blood..." He looked at Ethan and the girls, who smiled encouragingly at him, and shrugged. "I like it here. I enjoy leading the treks. Maybe Alec will keep me on?" He looked from Rose to Thomas, then shook his head. "Anyway, I'm telling you so we can get everything out in the open. I figured it was pretty hypocritical of me to be mad at you both for keeping things from us when I was doing the same." As he finished speaking, he turned to Amelie and widened his eyes at her.

Rose held her breath.

"I've been keeping something from you too," she said. "I quit my job. It was Jed's idea, but I went along with it because I thought we were going to start a family and that I could spend the time finally writing a novel. Except now I'm starting to think it was rather silly of me." Less emotional than Ben but clearly still a little shaken, Amelie straightened her shoulders and tucked her hair behind her ear. "I didn't tell you because... well, probably because I was embarrassed and felt like I'd made a huge mistake."

Rose looked at Thomas, who was nodding slowly. "Nothing is unfixable, Amelie," he said, clearly still reeling from what Ben had said, but reaching out to take his youngest daughter's hand. "There will be other jobs."

Amelie smiled at her father, then turned to look at Rose. What Rose wanted to say was, *You silly girl. Why would you do that after working so hard to get to where you were?* But that was probably precisely the reason Amelie had kept it from her in the first place. So instead, she said, "Your father's right. After the wedding, you can figure out what you want to do."

"*If* you still want to get married." Cat had spoken suddenly and loudly and was staring at her sister with a purposeful look on her face. "Because, at the risk of being thrown in the pool again..."

Rose frowned and looked from one daughter to the other – thrown in the pool?

"You don't *have* to do anything. You don't *have* to marry him, Amelie."

As Cat's words lingered in the centre of the table, a stillness settled on the others. Rose was studying Amelie's face, trying to read the thoughts that were flitting across it. No one spoke. Until Thomas said, "Your sister is absolutely right. You don't–"

"Dad, stop." Amelie's face had changed, and she was looking into the distance.

"No, Amelie, I think it's important that I say this. Of all people, I know what it's like to–"

"Dad. Stop." Amelie was pointing towards the stables. "What's that?"

"It looks like smoke," Rose murmured, standing up at the same time as Thomas.

"Is Jean having a bonfire?" Ben asked. "Surely it's not the right season for that?"

"That's not a bonfire." Thomas' expression had darkened. His jaw was set tightly, and his fists were clenched at his side. Before saying anything else, he broke into a run. "Call the fire department!" he yelled back at them, already halfway down the steps despite his limp.

Rose gripped the edge of the table. She could barely breathe. A fire? A fire on the ranch?

"Mum – come on..." Amelie was pulling her arm.

Cat, Ethan, and Ben had caught up with Thomas, overtaken him, and were almost at the pool already. Swallowing down the fear in her mouth, Rose began to move. "Go fetch Alec and Skye," she said. "Tell Alec to get all the guests to the fire point up here at the house. And bring Skye for the horses in case..." She couldn't bring herself to say, *In case they need medical help*, but she didn't need to; Amelie was already tearing down the path towards the guests' cabins.

Taking her phone from her pocket, Rose dialled 112 and

spoke in quick, faulty Italian to the operator who told her to stay contactable and to wait for help to arrive so she could direct them.

As Rose paced back and forth, desperate to run after the others, Nonna appeared from the kitchen. "I smell..." She stopped in her tracks and her hands flew to her chest. "Rose..." she whispered.

"I have to go. I can't just wait here." Rose pressed her phone into Nonna's hands. "The fire department is on its way. They'll need directing. Alec is getting the guests up here to the fire point."

"I will see to it," Nonna said, rolling up her sleeves as if she might attempt to tackle the blaze herself. "Go."

Steeling herself for what she was about to witness, Rose took a deep breath. Then she followed her family towards the fire.

35
AMELIE

AMELIE FOUND Skye and Alec before she even reached their cabin. Walking hurriedly towards the main house, Alec called out, "Amelie? We saw smoke. Is everything–" Seeing her wide eyes, he stopped.

"It looks like a fire. Alec, some guests are already up by the pool, but Mum says you need to wake the others and get them to the fire point at the front of the house. Check you've got everyone. And Skye..." she looked at the smoke-filled air above the stables, "we might need a vet."

"I'm coming," he nodded.

Barely looking back at Alec, Amelie took off beside Skye. He was fast, and she had never been much of a runner, but he matched her pace and stayed with her.

"I don't even know how..." she said, wishing she could screw her eyes shut and wake up from whatever they were about to be confronted with.

Skye didn't reply. His usually light green eyes looked as

if they had turned grey, his lips were set into a thin straight line, and he was moving as if he had one thought and one thought only – get to the horses, quickly.

As they approached the stables, thick plumes of smoke billowed towards them. While the boys were further down the track, Cat had slowed and was jogging beside their father. Several times, Dad stumbled. Eventually, Cat took his arm and let him lean against her.

Catching up with them, and letting Skye run past, Amelie took Dad's other arm and he grimaced as he tried to quicken his pace.

At the gate that opened into the yard, they stopped. The air was foggy with smoke. Ethan, Ben, and Skye were gripping the gate, transfixed by what was in front of them.

Flames – huge, crackling, white-orange flames – had engulfed the barn that stored their hay supplies and were eating their way through the wooden framework of the stable next to it.

"Get the horses out of the stables," Dad shouted, unlocking the gate and charging into the yard. "Now!"

Ben didn't hesitate. Straight away, he ran forward and began opening doors. Close behind him, starting with the stalls nearest to the barn, the rest of them followed suit, diving in and trying to calmly – but quickly – lead the horses out and down towards the bottom paddock.

As each animal was freed, it stepped into the yard with wide eyes, instinctively trying to hurry away from the danger. Holding onto Rupert's halter, Amelie whispered to him, "It's okay boy, come on, this way," then took hold of Shadow too and guided both horses away from the yard.

"I think that's it..." Her mother had joined them at the paddock and was panting as she shut the gate behind the last horse. "I think that's all of them."

But as they hurried back to the yard, they could hear squealing. "Dot..." Amelie whispered, looking at her mother. "We forgot Dot."

On the other side of the gate, Ben and Cat were throwing buckets of water at the barn, coughing and spluttering as the flames licked higher and higher into the sky.

"It's spreading too fast," Ben shouted. "Dot and Andante are still in there!"

Amelie's heart was pounding as she searched for Skye, her father, and Ethan.

"Where's your father?" Mum shouted above the hiss and snap of the flames.

With tears in her eyes, Cat pointed at the stable. "He went in. Ethan and Skye followed him."

As Amelie reached for her mother's hand, everything became suddenly fuzzy and too loud. Somewhere in the distance, she was sure she could hear sirens, but all she could see was smoke and flames. And then Mum let go of her.

"Come here," she was saying, grabbing hold of Cat and Ben and dragging them back towards the gate. "There's nothing you can do. Come away."

"Mum. We've got to try." Ben was resisting, but Mum grabbed him by the arms and looked straight into his eyes. "It is not worth it. Come *away*."

As Mum shepherded Ben towards a small cluster of trees opposite the yard, Amelie put her arm around Cat's waist and followed. They could still hear squealing. It was Dot. A high-pitched braying sound that told them he was terrified and in trouble.

After what felt like an eternity, as the four of them huddled together, three tall silhouettes emerged from the stable with the short, stout figure of Dot the donkey in between them.

Quickly, Ben rushed forward to usher Dot out of the yard and down to the paddock where the horses were waiting. Cat grabbed Ethan, and patted his back as he coughed, wheezed, and tried to find his breath. And Mum reached for their father, putting her hands on his cheeks and shouting, "You fool, Thomas Goodwin. What were you thinking?!"

But Amelie was watching Skye. He was bent double and wheezing. As sirens inched closer, she went to him and lightly placed her fingers on his shoulder. His shirt was warm and, when he looked up, his face was flushed, and his eyes were red.

"Andante," he whispered. "She's still in there."

Amelie turned to look at her father. At the same time as her mother, she saw the look on his face.

"Dad, no."

"Thomas, don't."

"Mister Goodwin–" Skye stepped forward. But Dad had already turned and was running back to the fire.

"Dad!" Amelie shouted. And then Skye was running too. Without thinking, she followed him.

"Amelie, Thomas, come back!" Mum was yelling, but the sound of the flames drowned her out.

In front of the stable, the heat was like nothing Amelie had ever felt. Skye and her father were racing towards it, and she could see them looking for a way in. Putting her arm over her mouth and ducking her head, she ran to them.

"Here," Dad was saying. "I think we can get through here—" But as he stepped into the one flame-less gap, there was a creak, and a snap, and a huge section of timber came crumbling down in front of them – obscuring him from view.

"Dad!" Amelie reached out as if she might physically be able to grab hold of him, even though she couldn't see him.

She expected Skye to charge forward, find a way through, and drag her father to safety. But when she looked at him, he was frozen. From head to toe, he was shaking. His breath was coming thick and fast, and he was grasping at his chest.

"Skye..." Amelie grabbed his hand and squeezed it. When he didn't respond, she put her palms on his cheeks. "Skye."

She was coughing. They both were. And as a second crash sounded from inside the stable, she tore her eyes away from the spot where her father had stood, and pulled Skye back towards the gate.

3 6
ROSE

WATCHING Amelie and Skye stumble towards her without Thomas, Rose clung to the gate as if she might fall down without it. Behind her, sitting on a bench beneath the trees, Ethan was still struggling to breathe, and Cat was crying.

Rose looked at Amelie, then Skye, then – before she could stop herself – let out a small mewing sound. "Thomas," she whispered. "What have you done? What have you done?"

"We couldn't get to him," Amelie said, coughing. Beside her, Skye was utterly mute, and seemed only to be moving because she was guiding him forward. "The roof caved in. We couldn't get him."

Rose reached for Amelie and pulled her close, kissing the top of her head and using the warmth of her daughter's body to calm herself. "It's okay. It's going to be okay."

Then, from the fire-lit path between the barn and the nearby field, Alec appeared. Close behind him, the wail of a fire engine followed. "The fire brigade's here," he shouted, gesturing for them all to move back from the gate as flashing blue lights merged with dancing orange shadows.

"Son?" Alec took hold of Skye and shook his shoulders. "Skye? Are you all right, son?"

When Skye didn't respond, Rose put a hand on Alec's shoulder and pointed towards the stable. "Thomas is in there," she said shakily. "Skye tried to go after him but..." She trailed off, biting back the huge painful sobs that were threatening to overwhelm her.

Two fire engines and an ambulance had come to a stop in front of the barn. Firefighters and paramedics poured out of them and swarmed around Rose and her family. Two women she hadn't seen before, who announced they were vets, asked where to find the horses.

Gesturing to the paddock, Rose said, "Skye's a vet too. He looked at them briefly as we moved them but–"

"We'll see to them, ma'am," the taller of the two women replied, already striding towards the paddock.

Rose turned back to the barn and swallowed hard. "My husband is in there," she whispered. Then, approaching the fire fighter who looked like he was in charge, she said again, louder this time, "My husband is in there. He went back for one of our horses."

"Mrs Goodwin? Stay here. We will deal with this," was the reply and, seconds later, as paramedics wrapped Ethan and Skye in crisp silver blankets and placed oxygen masks over their faces, huge jets of water began to spill out of the fire hoses and onto the flames.

Batting back the advances of the paramedics, Rose linked

arms with Amelie and Cat and stood stock-still, staring at the yard.

For what seemed like forever, nothing happened.

Rose was closing her eyes and whispering prayer after prayer under her breath when Cat gripped her hand. "Mum…"

Rose prised her eyes open. A huge black silhouette was emerging from the flames.

She held her breath.

The silhouette was moving towards them at lightning speed. "Andante…" she whispered.

"Look…" Cat had pulled away and was pointing. "On her back!"

Letting out a choked cry of utter relief, Rose ran towards the large black horse. Andante had made it through the gate but was now pacing up and down in front of the trees, looking as if she might bolt at any second. On her back, Thomas was slumped forward, his cheek resting against her thick black mane.

Waving back the paramedics, Rose gestured for quiet and slowly approached. "Andante," she whispered. "What a brave girl you are."

Andante was wheezing. Her eyes were wide, and she was scraping her right hoof on the floor. But she didn't run. She let Rose walk right up to her and put a hand on her nose.

"There," Rose whispered, stroking softly and watching from the corner of her eye as Ben inched forward and slipped a lasso around Andante's neck.

Nodding at the paramedics, Rose helped Ben hold Andante still as they eased Thomas down onto a stretcher.

"Take Andante down to the paddock," Rose said to Ben. "And tell the vets she needs special attention."

Ben nodded but lingered for a moment, looking at where the paramedics were poring over his father.

"Go on," said Rose. "He's okay. He's safe now." But when she looked at Thomas, his eyes were closed. She couldn't see his chest moving. She walked slowly towards him, her own heart frozen in her ribcage.

Ethan was standing beside the paramedics, watching them with wide eyes and nervous hands. And then, finally, Thomas spluttered. Coughed. Gasped for breath.

Rose's hands flew to her mouth, and she choked down a cry of relief. Her arms and legs felt suddenly heavy. She reached for her children. She wanted to feel them – to hold them close to her – but they were too far away. Her head was spinning. She blinked hard and tried to steady herself, but it was no use. "I don't feel too good," she whispered.

And then everything went black.

37
AMELIE

Six Hours Later

"How's your mum?" Skye asked, wrapping his hands around a mug of the sweet nutmeg tea that Nonna had been making in copious amounts all night.

On the horizon, the sun was coming up. Smoke still lingered in the air, and Amelie was certain she could feel the heat from the embers of the barn, even though she knew it wasn't possible from where they were.

After Mum fainted, both she and Dad had been whisked swiftly to hospital. Ethan had gone with them – as if he thought that, as a medical student, he could be useful – leaving Cat, Amelie, and Ben behind to manage the triage of the horses.

Amelie and Cat had been talking to the vets from town when Skye had appeared. As if nothing had happened, as if he hadn't frozen to the spot and been unable to speak for an hour, he had slipped into army mode and taken charge.

The vets had briefed him, then the three of them had set about treating the horses that were suffering from smoke inhalation while Ben, Amelie, and Cat took those who were okay to the disused stables at the furthest edge of the property.

It had taken five hours to get the blaze under control, and the firefighters were still down there with Ben and Cat. Amelie had been reluctant to leave them, but someone needed to check on the guests, so eventually – around three a.m. – she'd told them to keep her posted and made her way back to the house. Skye had followed her, and as they'd walked silently away from the stables, she had slipped her hand into his.

Now, several hours later, they sat side-by-side watching the sleepy and worried guests trail back to their cabins.

In the office, Alec was making calls. Jean was still up in the hills and needed to know what had happened, and Alec had offered to get in touch with Katie too and fill her in.

Noticing that her right arm was sore but trying to ignore it, Amelie refilled her mug from the pot on the table and nibbled at her lower lip. She had no idea how *Heart of the Hills* was going to manage treks, lessons, or incoming guests over the next few weeks. But for now, she was trying to simply thank the stars that everyone was okay.

Re-reading the text Ethan had sent her from the hospital, she said, "Mum's fine. Shock and smoke inhalation. But mainly shock."

"And your dad?"

"He's okay. But he hasn't woken up yet." Amelie exhaled slowly then coughed as the air caught her still inflamed chest. Despite holding her mug, her hands still felt shaky.

Smiling gently, Skye gestured for her to drink up, and Amelie closed her eyes as the lukewarm liquid soothed her throat.

After a moment's silence, however, he leaned forward and rested his forearms on his thighs. Lacing his fingers together, he looked up at Amelie. His dusty, curly hair had fallen across his forehead and, in the early morning light, his eyes looked brighter than usual. "I'm sorry, Amelie," he said solemnly, as if they'd been having an entirely different conversation. "For not telling you the truth about why Dad and I were here."

Amelie shook her head at him; after everything they'd been through in the past twelve hours, she couldn't possibly still be mad at him. "Skye, you've already apologised. You were in a difficult position, I understand that."

"I know. But I don't want you to think… I'd hate for you to think that I'd ever lie to you or hurt you."

Amelie studied Skye's face – he was sincere, and sad, and she hated seeing him look so truly upset.

Shrugging his shoulders as though he was trying to make things a little lighter, he added, "I'm sorry for the way I was back there too. When the barn collapsed, I–"

Realising what he was about to say, Amelie reached quickly for his hands and took them between her own. "You do *not* need to apologise for that. No way."

"Of course, I do. If it wasn't for Andante, your father may have–"

"And if you'd gone in there after him, you may have... so, there's no apology needed." She squeezed his fingers.

Quietly, stroking her palm with his thumb and staring at their entwined fingers, Skye muttered, "I just couldn't..." Then he cleared his throat and, a little louder, said, "PTSD. I've had therapy for it, but..." He smiled a rueful smile at her. "That's why I had to leave the Corps. Just can't seem to shift it."

Amelie slowly reached out and touched her index finger to the scar above Skye's eyebrow. He leaned into her and it made her want to wrap her arms around him. The now-familiar scent of his aftershave had mixed with the smell of the smoke that was woven into his clothes, his skin was tinged with ash, and his eyes were tired. But when he looked at her, she knew it wasn't the heat of the embers making her cheeks flush.

"Skye..." Her words caught in her throat, but she forced them out. "When I saw you coming out of the fire with Dot, and my dad, and Ethan... I don't think I've ever been so happy in my life."

Skye didn't smile, didn't move, just watched her – holding his breath as if he was scared that she would stop speaking.

"The past few weeks..." Amelie closed her eyes. When she opened them again, she said, "These past few weeks, I've loved spending time with you. Probably a bit too much."

She stopped and scanned Skye's face for a clue that might betray what he was feeling. "Amelie..." He tilted his head. "I've loved spending time with you too. And if things were different..." He breathed in slowly, biting his lower lip. "If things were different, and you weren't engaged–"

"If I wasn't engaged, then...?" Amelie looked up at him, desperate for him to say what she couldn't.

Gingerly, Skye brushed her smoke-tinged hair behind her ear. "Then..." He put his hand on her shoulder, moved his fingers slowly down her arm.

Amelie held her breath. But as Skye's hand grazed her forearm, she felt herself wince. Unwillingly, she made a small *argh* sound and took her arm back.

The spell broken, Skye frowned at her. "Are you hurt?"

"It's nothing," she said quickly, meeting his eyes and willing him to say whatever he'd been on the cusp of saying.

"Let me see?" Skye carefully rolled up the sleeve of her blouse.

Amelie bit back a sharp stinging sensation as the fabric brushed against her skin.

"You've burned yourself." Skye took hold of her arm very lightly, being careful not to let his fingertips touch the burn itself. "When did you do this? Why didn't you show the paramedics?"

"I don't know," Amelie said, shaking her head. "I mean, I don't know when I did it. I didn't even realise it hurt until a little while ago."

"We need to get it seen to. They're still on standby down with the fire guys. I'll call Cat and ask her to send them up."

"There's really no need. I'm sure if I put some cream on it, it'll be fine." Amelie was deeply annoyed at herself. The magic of a few moments ago had dissolved, and she desperately wanted it back. She wanted to know how Skye felt about her – she *needed* to know how he felt. Because ever since they'd sat beside one another on the plane, she'd been denying that there was anything between them. But now, after being forced to think about how she'd feel if she lost him, she knew it was no use. When she was with Skye, she felt free, and alive, and whole, and calm, and excited all at the same time. Jed had never made her feel that way. *No one* had ever made her feel that way.

"Skye–"

But Skye was already taking his phone from his pocket and turning away from her.

"Cat? How's it going? Aha. Good. Listen, could you ask the paramedics to come up to the house? Nothing major – Amelie's got a burn that needs looking at. Thanks."

When Skye hung up, he paused. Their knees were almost touching. His eyes flitted to her engagement ring and Amelie swallowed hard. She wanted to say, *I don't want to marry him. I'm going to call it off. The whole thing.* But before she could, her phone rang.

"It's Aunt Katie," she said, in barely a whisper. "Your dad must have got through to her. I better–"

"Sure. I'll go wait for the paramedics." Skye stood up slowly, stopped – as if he was about to say something – then simply smiled a slow *it'll be okay* smile at her, and turned away.

38
ROSE

FOR THE SECOND time in as many years, Rose sat beside her husband's hospital bed with her fingers laced together in prayer, whispering again and again, "Please, let him be okay. Please, let him be okay."

Outside in the corridor, Ethan was pacing up and down. He was on the phone, and the way he was speaking made Rose lean closer to Thomas and whisper, "You know, I think Ethan has a girlfriend. You should ask him about it when you wake up. He's always talked to you more than he's talked to me. Especially about girls." As she spoke, she choked back a sob and bent to rest her forehead on Thomas' chest.

For at least a minute, she didn't move. She just listened to the beating of his heart and felt the warmth of his body against her cheek.

"You smell good..." Thomas' voice made her sit bolt upright.

Wiping tears from her cheeks, she said, "I smell of smoke and horses."

"Like I said... good." Thomas smiled at her.

Rose tutted, but she was smiling. "Andante–"

"Andante saved me," Thomas said croakily. "Darned horse wouldn't leave. My leg gave way. Didn't think I'd make it out, so I tried to shoo her through where it was safe." Thomas tried to push himself up to lean against his pillows, but was clearly struggling, so Rose stood up to help him. "She was amazing, Rose. She knelt down in front of me. I heaved myself onto her back..." He closed his eyes, and Rose wondered if he was trying to block out the sound and smell of the fire as the stables had collapsed around him. "I don't remember much else... is she okay?"

Rose nodded quickly. "She's fine. Skye and the vets from town triaged all the animals. No casualties. Although I think some will need rest for a few days, or weeks..." She trailed off, trying not to worry about how they'd manage the guests and the treks from now until the end of the season.

As if he could read her mind, Thomas squeezed her hand in his and said, "Don't worry. We'll sort it out. We've come through worse."

At that, Rose frowned. "Have we?"

"Well..." Thomas met her eyes then started to laugh. "Actually, no, I think this is probably as bad as it gets."

Rose pursed her lips and watched the smile she'd known for over half of her life light up her husband's face. And by the time Ethan stuck his head around the door to see what was happening, she was laughing too.

"Mum? Dad? Are you okay? What's so funny?"

"Nothing," Rose said, clasping her chest as she began to cough. "Nothing at all."

"Which is what makes it so..." Thomas was coughing now too.

"Funny," they said in unison.

39
AMELIE

AFTER SPENDING the rest of the morning fielding questions from the guests, Amelie, Cat, and Ben finally admitted defeat. The three of them were exhausted. Amelie's arm was still hurting and being in close proximity with Skye – who'd refused to return to his cabin despite Alec trying to persuade him to – was making her feel woozy.

"I'll handle it," Alec assured them. "Seriously. Go get some sleep. Katie will be here in an hour or so. Jean's almost back. And you'll be no use to man or beast if you pass out and get carted off to hospital to join your parents."

"All right," Cat said. "Come on, guys. Alec's right."

"Yes, he is," said Nonna, who'd been following them around with a deeply concerned look on her face all morning.

"You need some sleep too, Nonna." Amelie put her hand on the old woman's shoulder. "You're not superhuman."

At first, Nonna looked like she was going to protest. But

when a yawn enveloped her, she smiled, shrugged, and said, "I make a deal. You rest. I rest."

Amelie smiled and looked at Cat and Ben. "Okay. Deal." She leaned in and kissed Nonna's cheek. "See you in a few hours."

As the three of them headed back into the house from the veranda, Skye followed. But at the steps, he stopped. Gesturing towards his and Alec's cabin, he looked at Amelie. "I'm glad your arm's okay. See you soon."

"Yes," she said, a little stiffly. "See you soon."

Upstairs, Ben ducked into his room and closed the door, Cat went to shower, and Amelie flopped down on her bed and looked up at the ceiling. Blinking slowly, she tried to find the momentum to get up and use her mum's en suite to wash the smoke from her skin, and clothes, and hair. But before she'd even formulated the thought properly, she was asleep.

When she woke, it was to the sound of people chattering outside on the veranda. Slowly opening her eyes, Amelie turned towards the window. It was darker. Twilight.

She reached for her phone and was checking for messages from Ethan or her parents when there was a knock on her door. She looked up as Cat entered. In pyjamas, she padded in and sat down on the edge of Amelie's bed.

"What time is it?" Amelie asked, fighting back a yawn.

"Seven p.m." Cat yawned too. "We were asleep for hours. Mum and Dad are back, and Aunt Katie's here."

"Darn," Amelie said, sitting up straight but feeling a bit light-headed as she did so.

"It's okay. Alec's been great. He and Jean called *The Pines* and they're going to pitch in and help. Old man Rollo said that we'd do the same for him. Didn't hesitate, apparently."

A small notch of tension dissolved from her chest, and Amelie's shoulders relaxed a little. "Thank goodness."

"*And...*" said Cat, crossing one leg over the other and twirling a strand of hair between her fingers, "Bea's place offered to feed the guests tonight, so we don't have to worry. Pretty much everyone in *Legrezzia* clubbed together and arranged for a bunch of cars to come collect them."

Amelie's heart was throbbing – in a good way. "I forgot how great the people around here can be," she said, smiling.

"I know," Cat agreed. "Bea even sent food up for us, so Nonna didn't have to cook."

At the mention of food, Amelie felt suddenly and fiercely starving. Her stomach lurched into a loud growl that made Cat laugh.

"Me too," she said. "We haven't eaten for, what? Twenty-four hours."

"Something like that." Amelie stood up and walked to the window. Turning her back to it, she leaned against the sill and pushed her hands through her hair. It felt greasy and smelled awful. "I need to shower."

"Yes. You do." Cat stood up too and gestured to the door. "I'll go down. Just put your PJs on. No need for formalities this evening."

Amelie nodded then, fiddling with the hem of her blouse, added quietly, "Who's going to be at dinner?"

Cat, who was at the door, stopped and turned back towards her. "You mean is *Skye* going to be at dinner?"

Amelie met her sister's eyes, contemplated denying it, but then buried her face in her hands. "Yes."

Cat stepped back towards her, prised Amelie's fingers away from her eyes, and pointed to the bed. "Sit. And tell me what's going on."

"Nothing." Amelie sat down and tucked her knees up under her chin, looping her arms around them and hugging them close.

Cat tilted her head.

Releasing her breath, Amelie placed her forehead on her knees, waited a moment – hoping the thud-thud-thud of her heart would calm down – then looked at her sister. "I have feelings for Skye." The words came out quicker and easier than she'd expected, but she remained still as she waited for Cat's response.

After a few seconds, in which she looked at Amelie with a curious nose-wrinkled look on her face, Cat's lips spread into an enormous grin. "Ha!" she said, waving her arms. "At last!"

Amelie frowned.

"You two have been falling for each other ever since you arrived. I just didn't think you'd admit it."

"Cat..." Amelie's heart was jittering; someone else had noticed the chemistry between her and Skye. It wasn't just in her head. Even though they hadn't said it out loud – she hadn't been imagining it. But as she smiled, Jed's face flashed in front of her eyes. "I'm *engaged*," she said, her smile dropping as Jed's name danced round and round in her head.

Tutting, and flicking her hand as if the wedding that was due to take place in a few days' time was totally inconsequential, Cat replied, "Yes. And?" When Amelie didn't respond, she shook her head, inched forward, and put her hands on Amelie's knees. "Listen, I'm not saying that whatever's going on with Skye is a reason to call off the wedding. If you were madly in love with Jed, I'd tell you to just keep your mouth shut and get down that aisle. I'd tell you that whatever you feel for Skye is probably just a crush, one last flirt with freedom, and that when you get back to England after the wedding Skye will fade into nothing but a nice memory."

Amelie's mouth was dry, and her tongue felt three sizes too big for her mouth.

"But..." Cat pressed down lightly on Amelie's knees. "I don't think you are madly in love with Jed. And I think you know that."

Amelie blinked and looked up at the ceiling. A small thin crack that she hadn't noticed before led from the window frame to the light fitting and, as tears filled her eyes, it wavered. "The thought of going back to England..." She forced herself to look at Cat. Then she sniffed loudly and wiped her nose with the back of her hand. "But it's not just because I'd miss Skye. I'd miss you, and Mum, and Ben, and this place. And I just..." She began to cry, her words coming out in short, sharp bursts between sobs as she said what she'd been holding inside for weeks. "I just don't think I really love Jed."

Without missing a beat, Cat pulled Amelie close. Squeezing her tight, she kissed her forehead then sat back to look at her. "There," she said, smiling. "That's the worst part over. You've admitted it." Smiling again and wiping a tear from Amelie's cheek, Cat nodded firmly. "Now you just need to tell him."

"Which one?" Amelie sniffed.

"Well," Cat said, "both of them."

40
ROSE

KATIE AND ALEC had lit the veranda with small soft lanterns, pushed three tables together, and arranged Bea's food in the centre of it. When Rose stepped outside and saw it, relief washed over her; they were safe. All of them. The horses were okay. The children were okay, and Thomas was okay. Whatever happened next, for tonight, this was all that mattered.

Ben, Ethan, and Thomas were already seated. The doctors hadn't been happy about Thomas leaving, but he had insisted that Ethan could keep an eye on him, and they were now chatting quietly with a softness between them that Rose had so dearly missed seeing.

Sheepishly, Ethan showed Thomas something on his phone and Thomas clapped him on the back. Rose was certain now that Ethan had met a girl, and she vowed to prod Thomas about it later on; she hated being left out of things like that, but Thomas always seemed to be the one 'in the know' about their kids' love lives.

As Rose stood watching them, Katie stepped up beside her and looped her arm through Rose's.

"Thank you for this," Rose said, pressing close against her best and oldest friend.

"I'm so glad you're all okay," Katie replied. "I don't know what I'd do if I lost any of you."

Sitting down side-by-side, they each poured themselves a glass of wine and Rose smiled as Nonna and Alec joined them too. "Just the girls and Skye," Alec said, "and then we're all here."

"Here they are." Rose waved at her daughters as they emerged from inside. They were both wearing pyjamas and Amelie had damp hair, but Rose couldn't believe how beautiful they were. Taking the empty seat beside her, Amelie turned to Rose and gave her a big, tight hug.

"I'm so glad you're all right," Amelie said. Sitting back, she looked across the table at her father. "You too, Dad. I honestly thought–"

But Thomas cut her off by gesturing to the food in front of them. "For the first time in forever," he said, "we're all at the same table. So, despite what brought us here, let's enjoy it – okay?" Looking purposefully around the table with a familiar twinkle in his eyes, Thomas raised his glass. And as everyone else raised theirs too, Skye appeared from inside.

He sat down opposite Amelie and lifted his own empty glass to say, "Cheers." But as her family helped themselves to food and slipped into low, simple conversation, something snagged in Rose's mind; something wasn't right between

Skye and Amelie. They weren't looking at each other. And Cat was looking at the pair of them a little *too* much.

Telling herself to ignore it, Rose rested her elbows on the table and concentrated on the warm, content feeling in her belly as she watched the people she loved most in the world, all in the same place, talking, and eating, and laughing.

They'd finished their food, were all yawning, and were gratefully accepting mugs of strong coffee from Nonna when the sound of a car's engine in the distance made them look up. The guests weren't due to arrive back from *Legrezzia* yet, and they weren't expecting any arrivals this evening.

Just beyond the front of the house, headlights appeared. Thomas looked at Rose, but she shrugged.

"I'll go see who it is," he said, stiffly getting up from the table.

The others turned back to their drinks. Alec was telling them about the plans he, Jean, and Rollo had put in place, and Ben was nodding approvingly. "I'll help come up with a timetable for everything tomorrow," he said.

Even though Rose was focussed on watching Thomas' tired gait as he walked towards the steps, she couldn't help but notice the tone in Ben's voice; he was trying to impress Alec. When he told them that he'd known about Thomas' gambling problem from the very beginning, he said that he enjoyed working on the ranch more than training to be a doctor and that he was hoping Alec would keep him on after the sale went through.

Rose swallowed down a sigh and made a mental note to ask Alec herself. If he didn't think it was workable, she'd try Rollo. Wondering whether Alec might also agree for Cat to keep working on reception for a while, Rose narrowed her eyes in Thomas' direction. Whoever had arrived, Thomas was greeting them with a pat on the shoulder and gesturing for them to follow him back to the table.

When Thomas and his companion reached the edge of the veranda, and the lanterns lit their faces, Rose turned slowly to her daughter. "Amelie," she said, "you have a visitor..."

AMELIE

AMELIE PUT her mug down on the table so quickly that coffee sloshed over the edge. She could feel Skye watching her and – as she watched Jed walk confidently towards them – her cheeks burned.

"Surprise," he said loudly, sweeping his arms around her waist and pulling her to her feet.

"What are you doing here?" Amelie stiffly hugged him back. "You said you'd be in Pisa until Friday."

Jed brushed his fingers through his thick floppy hair and smiled at her. His movie star smile. "What can I say?" He looked at the others as he spoke. "I missed her too much." A quizzical look passed over his face. "And that leaning tower isn't nearly as interesting as it seems in the pictures. Once you've seen it online... well, that's it really, isn't it?" Jed chortled as he spoke, and Amelie felt herself cringe at the poshness of his accent.

At the table, her family looked surprised, intrigued, and

amused in equal measures. Finally, Mum told Ben to fetch Jed a chair and invited Jed to join them.

Jed nodded, then nudged Amelie's side with his elbow. "Are you going to introduce me, babe?"

Amelie daren't look at Cat; she knew her sister would be biting back bile at the sound of that awful nickname. "Of course." One-by-one, she pointed at everyone and said their names. "And this is Alec Anderson–"

"Ah, the chap who's buying the ranch." Jed nodded approvingly. "Jolly good deal for you, hey?"

Alec smiled thinly. "I'm excited about it, yes."

"So, you must be...?" Jed narrowed his eyes at Skye as if he truly had no idea who he might be.

Come to think of it, Amelie wasn't sure whether she'd ever mentioned Skye to Jed; probably, she hadn't. "Skye," Amelie said, her tongue thickening at the feel of his name. "Alec's son. He's going to help run the place when the sale's gone through."

Hesitantly, she looked at him. But when their eyes met, she wished she hadn't.

"Well," Jed said, clapping his hands, "before I sit down and finally get acquainted with you all, I have a surprise."

Amelie's stomach tightened. "Jed, I'm not sure now's the time. We've had a difficult twenty-four hours–"

But Jed seemed totally oblivious to the fact that Amelie and Cat were in pyjamas, or that smoke was lingering in the air, or that there were no guests anywhere to be seen. "Sorry, Amelie. I simply can't wait any longer to tell you."

At the table, Ethan quipped, "If he was a woman, I'd be pretty sure he was about to announce he was *with child*."

Ben and Cat giggled but, shooting them a *please be polite* look, their mother graciously smiled at Jed. "Go ahead, we can fill you in on events later. And it sounds like whatever you've got to tell Amelie is important."

Straightening himself up as if he was about to deliver a keynote speech at a conference, Jed adjusted his collar and cleared his throat.

Amelie was still standing and felt horribly uncomfortable. Her arm was stinging, her legs were so tired they felt like jelly, and she could feel Skye's presence nearby.

"Amelie," Jed said purposefully. "These past few months, since we got engaged, I've been a jerk." He waved his hand at her as if he thought she might protest. "No, seriously, I have been. I brushed you off when you wanted to show me houses. I refused to talk about trying for a baby—"

"Jed—" Amelie's skin was crawling.

"No, it's okay, I won't embarrass you." Jed took her hands between his and smiled at her – the way he had when he proposed all those months ago. "But I am going to explain. You see, the reason I was behaving so badly is that I was keeping a pretty big secret."

As Jed spoke, Amelie held her breath.

Slowly, he reached into his pocket and took out his phone. Swiping it open, he handed it to her. "Here," he said, grinning. "*This* is the secret."

Amelie blinked hard and tried to focus on the image on the screen. "The house in Epping... but this went off the market months ago. We looked at it back in—"

"I know!" Jed put his hands on her shoulders and dipped to meet her eyes. "It went off the market because I bought it."

Lightheadedness made Amelie sway gently from foot to foot. "You *bought* it?"

"For you! As a wedding present." Turning to the others and passing the phone to Amelie's father, Jed said, "She fell in love with it, but I pretended I wasn't interested. I wanted it to be a surprise. It's got everything – a big garden, hardwood floors, original fireplaces – and it's a stone's throw from the train station."

Amelie curled her fingers around the back of her chair to steady herself. Panic was rising in her chest like it had in the dress shop. She could feel her breath quickening.

"Babe? You do still love it?" Jed touched her forearm, and she bit her lower lip as his fingers pressed against her injury. The feeling of it brought nausea to her throat.

"Of course, I do."

"I think," her father said loudly, "she's just overwhelmed. But, well done, Jed. Wonderful gesture."

Jed was smiling, but Amelie could feel Skye watching her. He was standing up, moving towards her and, as she wavered, he caught her.

"You almost passed out." Cat was sitting on the end of the sofa, watching Amelie sip at her tea while their mother perched on the coffee table, purposefully not asking any questions.

"I know."

"He bought you a house." Cat raised her eyebrow.

"I know."

"Skye *caught* you as you passed out."

"I didn't pass out. I *nearly* passed out."

"But still..."

Amelie looked down into her tea. "I know."

Finally, Mum spoke. "Girls, is there something going on here that I should know about? Because I can brush this off as Amelie being overwhelmed, excited, exhausted... any of it. But I feel like there's something else happening." Looking from one to the other, she added, "I know I've been preoccupied lately but I'm still your mother and it's my job to help you fix things if there's a problem. So, is there a problem? With the wedding? With Jed?"

Amelie tapped her fingers on the side of her mug. Why not just say it? *I'm falling for Skye. I'd decided not to marry Jed. But now he's bought me a house, and I don't know what to do.* But she couldn't. How could she possibly say that she was having doubts now that everything she thought had been wrong between them had, in fact, been a misunderstanding? She thought Jed had been distant. She thought he'd changed his mind about wanting a family and about buying a house. But actually, the entire time, he'd been preparing to give her the biggest gift of her life.

Looking at Cat as she spoke, imploring her with her eyes not to say anything, Amelie answered her mother's question. "There's no problem. I'm just tired from last night. Everything's fine."

Cat opened her mouth to speak, but Amelie repeated slowly, "Everything is fine. Everything is fine."

42

ROSE

Three Days Later

IT WAS mid-morning and Rose was sitting on the porch swing watching a team of events co-ordinators manage the putting up of a large white marquee in the space between the veranda and the pool. The wedding was less than twenty-four hours away. Guests had been arriving from England since yesterday and, despite most of them staying at B&Bs in *Sant Anna*, they had been popping up in clusters every few hours to look at the ranch, greet Amelie and Jed, and introduce themselves to the family.

Spotting Alec on the path from the stables, Rose waved. He waved back and quickened his pace until he was standing in front of her.

"It got busy around here," he said, gesturing to where Cat and Amelie were directing Ethan to string fairy lights along the hedges by the pool.

"It did," Rose said. "How are things with the horses?" Over the last few days, she and Thomas had willingly allowed Alec to step in and help manage things. He was keen, had more energy than they did after everything they'd been through in the past eighteen months, and would soon be in charge of the place anyway. So, it made sense.

"Good. We've made some adjustments to the old stables down the far end of the paddocks. They'll be perfectly good until we can repair the fire damage. Although..." he rubbed his chin and narrowed his eyes thoughtfully, "I think it'll be a case of a total re-build. Not much to salvage, I'm afraid."

Shifting in her seat, Rose nodded. "The insurance will pay out for whatever's necessary," she said. "The fire department confirmed it was an accident – dodgy wiring in the barn – so, I just need to send over the paperwork."

"Great." Alec smiled as if he hadn't really been that worried about the insurance anyway.

Turning towards him, Rose took a deep breath then brushed her hands over her lap and said, "Listen, Alec. If you're still happy to go ahead with the purchase–"

"Of course, I am," Alec said firmly.

Rose nodded, relief allowing her jaw to unclench. "Then I was wondering if you'd consider keeping Ben on your staff. I know we discussed Nonna–"

"Oh, you've no worries there. Her food is unbeatable."

"But Ben..." Rose was struggling to find the right words. Since the fire, she'd felt exhausted – like all the stress and trauma of recent months had sunk into her bones and the only way to process it was to move, speak, and think very slowly indeed. "He loves working here. He gave up his medical career to help me, and–"

"Of course, he can stay." Alec crossed one leg over the other and rubbed at his chin again. "In fact..." He looked at her from the corner of his eye and the hint of a smile crossed his lips. "I was hoping that a few members of staff might stay on."

"You were?" Rose leaned her back into the cushion behind her. "That's great."

"Jean, of course. Nonna and Ben. Cat – if she wants to, she's been a whizz on reception – and..." Alec paused, angling himself so that his arm was resting on the back of the swing. "And you, Rose. You and Thomas."

Rose blinked hard. Her ears had gone fuzzy, and she felt as if she was underwater staring up at a too-bright sun. "I'm sorry?" She must have misheard him; she should probably go and lie down.

"I love this place." Alec waved his hand at the landscape in front of them. "Della would be just so happy to think that this is what I chose to do with her legacy and with my own – useless before now – money. I've seen how happy Skye's been since we got here and I think, for both of us, it's the fresh start we need. But we're still learning the ropes."

"Jean and Ben will help with that," Rose said, suddenly terrified that Alec was about to back out. Change his mind. Leave her plummeting back to square one, except now with a burned down barn and a long wait for the insurance money to fix it.

"I know. But Rose, you and Thomas are the beating heart

of this place. It wouldn't be *Heart of the Hills* without the both of you."

"Alec, please don't." Rose closed her eyes.

"Which is why I'd like you to stay on after the sale goes through. I'd own the business, but you and Thomas could still manage the day-to-day, teach me what's what, help Skye get to grips with it all." Looking up at the house, Alec said, "You can stay here, your kids can stay. Nothing has to change."

Rose's mouth was sandpaper dry. Placing her fingers over her throat, she swallowed hard. "You're asking us to *stay*?"

"I am. If you think that kind of arrangement could work?"

Before Alec could finish speaking, Rose flung herself towards him. Wrapping her arms around his neck, she began to laugh. "Alec Anderson, you are probably the kindest, loveliest man I've ever known. *Of course*, we'll do it. Of course, we'll stay."

As she unwound herself from him and shuffled backwards, Rose couldn't stop herself from grinning.

"You think Thomas will agree?"

Rose's grin faltered, but only for a moment. And this time, when she said, "Yes, he will," she meant it with every fibre of her being.

43
THOMAS

"HOW'S SHE DOING?" Thomas winced as he sat down on one of the benches opposite the paddock. Skye was standing by the fence watching Andante.

"Good. She's an incredible horse."

Thomas nodded in agreement; she was incredible. He'd known it from the day he met her. "Certainly is," he said.

Moving away from the fence, Skye sat down beside him and took a long swig from the bottle of water he'd been holding. Since the fire, Thomas had noticed that Skye had been spending more time with the horses than with the other kids and, although he was impressed by the young vet's compassion for the animals, he had a feeling it was to do with more than just a concern for the horses' welfare.

"You doing okay, son?" Thomas looked ahead as he spoke. "I heard you had a tough time in the Middle East, and something like this..." he gestured towards the blackened carcass of the barn, "it can bring back memories."

Thomas had never served in the army, had never fought or trained as a soldier, and had never wanted to. But he knew people who had. And he also knew what it was like to experience trauma. Although he hadn't admitted it at the time, his accident had affected him mentally as well as physically, and he knew now that he'd waited far too long before reaching out for help.

"It was tough for a moment there, Sir, but I got through it." Skye's answer was formal, curt, as if he was speaking to a superior officer.

Thomas nodded. "You were in the Veterinary Corps?"

"Yes, sir. They paid for my veterinary training and then I signed up as part of a canine unit." Slowly, he stood up and walked a few feet away to lean against the trunk of a large oak tree. "We were scoping out an abandoned insurgents' camp." He swallowed hard. "The dogs went in first, but it was booby-trapped. We lost them all. One of them, Dallas, I'd raised her from a pup. She tried to make it out, but..." Skye closed his eyes, then looked at Thomas. "When the barn came down in front of you..."

Thomas pursed his lips. "I see," he said. "Is this the first time you've talked about it?"

"I had some therapy. Didn't like it too much." Skye tried to smile, but it didn't reach his eyes.

"Well," said Thomas, putting his hands firmly on his thighs and trying to channel the confident, worldly wise father figure he'd been back before his accident, "I certainly understand what it's like to have your identity taken away. Leaving the Army, it's a huge shift. You have to recalibrate. And it's hard."

Skye was focussing on Andante.

Thomas stood up and placed a firm hand on his shoulder. "It takes time. And, heck, I made a complete mess of it. When I was told I couldn't ride anymore, I didn't know who I was. This place, and the horses, was my life. But trust me, keeping it all bottled up inside – that helps no one. Even if you think the people around you don't want to hear about it, it's better for them and for you if you tell them what's going on up here." Thomas tapped his temple with his index finger. Then he squeezed Skye's shoulder, said, "And that's the lecture over with," and left him alone with his own thoughts.

44
AMELIE

FOR THREE DAYS, Jed had barely left her side. He seemed giddy with excitement. So much so that he hadn't even batted an eyelid when she told him about only ordering enough of the expensive champagne to cover the speeches instead of the main meal.

His triumph at successfully surprising her with the house hummed on his skin, and he was clearly trying extra hard to ingratiate himself to her parents and her siblings. He had even headed out for a ride with her, despite his ambivalence towards horses. And the whole thing was making Amelie feel sick to her stomach.

Three mornings in a row, she'd woken up praying that the feeling would be gone. Each day, for a brief glimpse of time, as she looked at the light beyond the window and at her childhood bedroom, she'd felt calm. But as soon as she set her feet down on the cool wooden floor, a creeping, prickly sense of uneasiness gripped hold of her once again.

She had tried to conjure up a feeling of excitement. She had spent hours before going to sleep looking at photographs of the house in Epping and trying to imagine herself living there. Jed had already drawn up plans to convert the garage into a studio for her to write in, and he had delighted in telling her that Hugh and his wife lived just a short train ride away. "We can have dinner parties, and there's plenty of room for your parents to come and stay," he'd said, brimming with pride. "And the third bedroom will be perfect as a nursery."

A few months ago, that thought would have filled Amelie with joy. But something had happened when she got on the plane from London. Something inside her – and between them – had shifted. And the woman who had wanted an old Victorian town house on the outskirts of London, and a husband who wore a suit every day, and lavish holidays in Bali, seemed like a stranger to her.

As she thought about the house Jed had bought, loneliness scratched at her insides. London felt too far away, too grey, and too sombre. The total opposite of the ranch.

And now, looking at Jed as he pitched in to help erect the marquee, she imagined doing what her father had done – taking the car in the middle of the night and driving off somewhere hidden, somewhere no one could find her.

"Am? Is this right?" Ethan was on a stepladder in front of the veranda, looping fairy lights through the railings. "Amelie?" he repeated sharply.

"Yes, fine," she said, barely looking at him. "Have you seen Skye?"

She heard Ethan tut loudly and caught him rolling his

eyes at her. "No, I haven't. But Alec said something about him going for a ride."

"A ride?" Amelie looked at her watch. "When was this?"

After climbing down from the stepladder, Ethan folded his arms in front of his chest. "I don't know. But I do know that you need to talk to him. You can't carry on like this. You're getting married in twenty-four hours and you look like it's a funeral you're planning for."

Amelie opened her mouth to protest, but then closed it again. "I'll be back," she said, already starting off in the direction of the stables. "Tell Jed I'll be back soon."

At the stables, Jean told Amelie that Skye left for the creek over an hour ago. Without thinking, suddenly fiercely desperate to see his face after several days of barely catching a glimpse of him around the ranch, she saddled up Rupert and set off in pursuit.

It was a slow journey. She wanted to break into a canter and make it across the meadow a little quicker but knew she shouldn't make Rupert exert himself so soon after the fire. Eventually, though, the creek came into view and Amelie spotted Shadow standing beneath the trees.

"Skye?"

He was sitting on the riverbank and turned to look at her. He didn't get up, so she left Rupert beside Shadow and walked over to him.

"Jean said I'd find you here."

Skye looked at his watch. "It's three o'clock. Your rehearsal dinner is–"

"Hours away." Amelie batted her hand at the air and sat down a few feet away from him. Crossing her legs, she picked a blade of grass and began to turn it between her fingers. "I haven't seen you much," she said finally, unable to stand the silence any longer. "Since Jed arrived."

Skye looked away, and his eyes drifted towards a spot on the opposite side of the river.

"Have you been avoiding me?" She was trying to sound light-hearted but could hear the twinge of disappointment in her voice.

"No." Skye shook his head and brushed his hair back from his face to expose the scar that she now knew like the back of her hand. "I've been giving you space, that's all."

Amelie bit her lower lip and drummed her fingers on her knee. "What if I don't want space?"

As her words hung in the air between them, Skye closed his eyes. "I can't do this," he whispered.

Amelie rubbed the back of her neck. It was warm, even beneath the shade of the trees, and there was no breeze to cool her. "What do you mean?"

"I can't pretend I'm okay with watching you get married." He turned and allowed his eyes to graze hers. "Until Jed arrived, I didn't have to think about it too much. In the beginning, I told myself it was in my head – the way I was feeling – thinking there was something between us. But after the fire..." He trailed off.

"It wasn't in your head." Amelie inched closer, willing the space between them to disappear.

"I know," he said. "And when I realised that, I thought maybe, just maybe, you'd call the whole thing off."

Amelie swallowed hard. His words stung her skin like hailstones in a storm.

Skye laughed ruefully and looked away. "But then your fiancé bought you a *house*, and he's not the uptight jerk I thought he'd be. Sure, he's a little irritating. But he seems like a good guy. And he loves you."

"Skye–"

"And now there's a marquee in front of the house, and a stage for the band, and guests from England, and fairy lights. And I can't stay and watch it, Amelie."

Amelie was biting back tears but knew she wouldn't keep them at bay for long.

Skye breathed in sharply through his nose so that his nostrils flared and his chest expanded. "So, I'm going to hide out here. Camp by the creek for a few nights. And when I go back down to the ranch, you'll be married and on your way to Bali, and I'll have pulled myself together." He moved his hand as if he was about to touch her, but didn't. "And the next time we see each other, we'll be friends."

"Friends?" Amelie wiped her tear-dampened cheek with the side of her hand.

"Good friends. Friends who see each other when you come visit from London. Friends who could have been something but who decided not to be."

45
AMELIE

ON THE DAY of the wedding, Amelie woke before sunrise, pulled on a large cream jumper, and walked slowly down to the pool. Everything was ready. The rehearsal dinner had gone well, her parents had looked happy, and Cat and the twins had been on good form. Even Jed's groomsmen hadn't been too obnoxious.

In typical Tuscan style, the wedding party had stayed up drinking red wine until close to midnight. But Amelie and Jed had retreated to their separate accommodation to get some rest.

She imagined that, in his cabin, Jed would have fallen asleep as soon as his head hit the pillow; rarely did he have trouble sleeping. But Amelie lay awake until the early hours of the morning, staring at the ceiling for what seemed like an eternity before she finally gave in and made her way downstairs.

Of course, the grounds in front of the house were empty.

The guests were all in their cabins. Even Nonna's cockerel hadn't raised its head yet.

At the pool, trying to empty her mind, Amelie sat down by the water and closed her eyes. Several times over the past few days, Cat had tried to corner her and speak to her about the wedding. But Amelie had brushed her off.

"He bought me a house, Cat," she'd said in hushed tones as her sister stepped in front of her. "Everything I thought was wrong between us was just him trying to surprise me. How can I abandon him after that?"

"But do you *love* him?" Cat had asked.

Amelie hadn't answered. Even now, as the question turned over and over in her mind, she didn't know the answer. She wanted to love him. Possibly, once they were lying on sun loungers in Bali, she'd remember why she had fallen for him when they first met. But what if she didn't? What if that feeling never came back?

Shaking her arms to free them from the tightness that seemed to be gripping her entire body, she breathed out slowly and looked up at the sky. It was brightening. The day was about to start.

Behind her, the sound of bare feet on the cool stone slabs made her heart skip a beat. "Skye?"

But when she turned, it wasn't Skye – it was her father. "Afraid not," he said, bending down stiffly so that he could sit beside her.

"You shouldn't–"

"I'm fine. Really. Fine." After a moment's silence, looking at the sky, he said, "It's early."

"Yes, it is."

"It's your wedding day."

"Yes," she said. "It is."

"But it doesn't have to be." Amelie daren't look at her father. As she tried to calm her breathing, he reached for her hand and squeezed it gently. "My darling girl, whatever you decide to do today, your family will be here to love you and support you."

She couldn't speak. There were words, so many words, but none of them would come out.

"I'm not sure I have much advice," Dad said.

Amelie tried to laugh. "That makes a change."

"But I will say this... Jo didn't marry Laurie, did she?"

"Jo?" Amelie was frowning at him; she'd no idea that he'd even read *Little Women,* let alone that he knew the characters' names.

"It was the hardest decision of her life. But she said no to him. And they were both happier for it, in the end."

46
ROSE

Rose was sitting in the kitchen, yawning into a mug of coffee, when Thomas appeared from outside. He walked in holding a small blue flask, the exact kind he'd brought her every single morning when they first met, and smiled at her. Looking down at his feet, he wiggled his eyebrows and Rose followed his gaze to see that he was wearing a pair of red cowboy boots.

"Not those old things," she said, shaking her head at him. "Not for a wedding, surely?"

"I wore them for our wedding." Thomas handed her the flask and, despite the fact she'd already got coffee, she took it from him.

"I know, but Jed's friends move in different circles from ours," Rose replied, smiling.

Thomas sat down opposite her and helped himself to one of the pastries Nonna had prepared the night before. "Listen, Rose," he said, after swallowing down a couple of mouthfuls and dusting off his hands. "Whatever happens today, with the wedding, I wanted to let you know that I've signed the paperwork."

Thomas' twinkling smile faded into something more serious as he took Rose's hands between his.

"You're right. Selling the ranch to Alec is the only way out of the mess I got us into."

Rose opened her mouth to speak – she'd been waiting until after the wedding to give Thomas the news that Alec wanted them to stay on as managers, keeping it close to her chest like a precious and glorious secret. But he kept on talking.

"I don't know what that means for us – Thomas and Rose – but I'd like to try to figure it out. Together." Sitting back and putting his hands into his lap, Thomas watched her closely.

"Thomas, I..." Rose stopped and frowned. "What do you mean? *Whatever happens today?*"

"Amelie hasn't said anything to you?"

Rose shook her head. "No. Why? What's wrong?"

"Well, in the interests of never keeping anything from you again..." Thomas leaned closer and lowered his voice conspiratorially. "I don't think she wants to marry Ted."

"*Jed,*" Rose corrected. Then blinked at him. "I *knew* there was something wrong. I asked the girls, but they wouldn't talk to me." A little incredulously, she added, "How is it that *you* know what's going on when I don't?"

Thomas smiled cheekily at her. "Well, because I've been learning to get in touch with my feelings. So, I spotted it a mile off."

"Spotted what?"

"Seriously, darling, you haven't noticed?"

"Noticed *what* Thomas?"

"That Amelie's in love with Skye. And that's she's definitely *not* in love with Ted."

"Jed."

"Exactly."

Rose looked at her phone for the time. The hair and makeup artist would be arriving any minute now to start beautifying Amelie and Cat. The dress, which Amelie had eventually returned to have properly fitted, was being steamed and carefully transported from the shop by Sofia. "Where is she?" Rose stood up.

"Still outside, I think. By the pool. But Rose–"

Whatever Thomas said, Rose didn't hear him. In flip flops, pyjamas, and a long grey cardigan, she jogged out of the house and down the steps. She needed to find her daughter because there was no way on Earth that she was going to let her marry a man she didn't love.

47
AMELIE

As she strode away from the pool and towards Jed's cabin, Amelie bumped headfirst into her mother.

"Amelie?" Mum gripped her upper arms. "Where are you going?"

"I—"

"Listen, I spoke to your father. I can't believe I didn't realise what was going on. But now I know, I can't let you go through with it. I can't let you marry Jed. Not if you're having doubts." Rose pressed her hands to Amelie's face and met her eyes. "Your wedding day should be the happiest day of your life. You shouldn't be looking like this. Sad, and anxious, and—"

"Mum?" Amelie almost smiled. "I know."

"You do?"

"I was on my way to speak to Jed." She looked at the path that led to the cabins.

"Oh." Mum let go of her and stepped back. "Oh, sweetheart."

"It's okay." A steely determination had settled in Amelie's stomach and she was refusing to let herself waver. "Really," she said. "It's okay."

"Can I do anything?"

"Wait up at the house to give me a hug when it's over?"

Mum nodded fervently. "I'll see you up there."

The walk from the pool to Jed's cabin took just a few minutes, but Amelie stood outside for much longer, steeling herself for what she was about to do.

Finally, she approached and knocked on the door.

"Am?" Jed looked tired. His hair was a mess, and he was squinting at her as if she'd disturbed him from a deep sleep.

"Jed. Can we talk?"

"Well," he blustered, "yes, but I thought it was bad luck to see the bride on the morning of the wedding?"

Amelie didn't answer, just ducked past him and positioned herself in the centre of the room. "Jed..."

He was watching her with sleepy eyes. "What is it, Amelie? You're worrying me."

Amelie didn't stop for breath. Without allowing herself to absorb the nervousness on his face or the droop of his mouth as she spoke, she said, "Jed, you're a wonderful man. You swept me off my feet from the second we met, and we had a lovely life together in London."

A wavering smile came to his lips.

"But – and this is the hardest thing I've ever had to say – I think maybe it all happened too quickly. I think we both got carried away with the idea of it but... I just don't think we're right for each other." Amelie blinked hard, willing herself not to cry. "I love that you've bought us a house, and that you're ambitious, and that you want to take care of me." She breathed in, forcing the air to fill her lungs. "But I don't think I love you anymore. And I'm so, so sorry. I hate myself for doing this to you, but it would be worse if I went through with it while I was feeling all these things and then told you afterwards. Wouldn't it?"

Jed wasn't moving. He was barely even blinking. "Went through with it?" His words came out slow and stunted. "Our wedding day is something you feel you have to *go through with*?"

Amelie pressed her lips together against the dryness of her mouth and closed her eyes. "I'm sorry."

"I bought us a house, Amelie."

"I know you did."

After a long fragile moment in which neither of them spoke, Jed suddenly let out a loud fierce growl and, turning to the nearby fireplace, swept a large vase of flowers onto the floor. Instantly, it shattered, sending splinters of glass shooting towards Amelie's bare feet.

Jumping back, she pressed herself against the wall, heart hammering. "Jed, I'm sorry–"

"Get out," he shouted, turning away from her. "Go! Leave!"

Amelie stretched her hand towards him. She wanted to

say something to make it better, but she knew there was nothing more to be said.

On the veranda, as she'd promised, Mum was waiting for her. Cat was there too, and Dad.

"I told Jed that I don't love him enough to marry him," she said, finally allowing the tears to come.

Without saying a word, her parents enveloped her in their arms. And then Cat's hand was squeezing hers. And the twins were there too, asking what was going on and being *shhh*'d by their mother as Cat offered a brief and abridged explanation.

"I'm sorry," Amelie muttered. "I'm so sorry to put you through all of this chaos." But as she came up for air and turned her blotchy face towards her family, Ben smiled at her.

"No use crying over uneaten wedding cake," he said softly.

"Yeah, he was pretty irritating, to be fair, Am," Ethan chimed in.

Nodding in agreement, Cat said, "I'll second that. Not our cup of tea."

As if she was about to give them each a clip around the ear, Mum batted her hand at them. But then Amelie started to laugh. The bubble of worry, and sadness, and fear that had been ballooning inside her day-by-day had popped. She felt desperately sorry for Jed, but she also felt free. Wonderfully free.

"Not mine either, as it turns out." She leaned into Cat and let her sister pull her close.

Patting her arm, Mum smiled. "I'm proud of you," she said. "But... what shall we do about the guests? They'll start arriving in a couple of hours."

Amelie swallowed hard; the thought of calling everyone and telling them the wedding was off made her feel more than a little queasy.

"Well, it's a shame to waste all this," Ethan said, waving at the marquee. "We tell them the wedding's off but to come and party, anyway. Surely?" He looked around at the others. They were watching Amelie.

"Am?" Cat nodded towards the marquee. "Do we tell them to come, anyway?"

Amelie thought of all the people who'd flown out from London, and of the fancy food, and the cheap wine, and the band that Cat had been so excited about. Straightening herself up and flicking her hair over her shoulders, she nodded. "Yes," she said. "We do."

48

ROSE

Leaning her upper half onto the open window frame, watching Cat and the twins dance erratically to the band's music, Rose sighed contentedly. Behind her, a floorboard creaked.

"Is that a contented sigh or a disappointed sigh?"

She knew it was Thomas even before he spoke and didn't turn to look at him. "Contented, actually," she said, a little sheepishly.

"You weren't a fan of Ted?"

"*Jed.*" Rose tutted, but she was laughing. "But no," she said as he stepped up beside her. "I wasn't a fan of him."

"Me neither, if I'm honest." Thomas smiled and, as their eyes met, it was as if no time had passed at all – as if they were still young, and in love, and waiting to start a new life together.

"Do you remember our wedding day?" Rose asked, almost without meaning to.

"Of course."

Rose inhaled slowly, then stood up and turned her back to the window. "I have some news about the sale."

Thomas visibly flinched.

"Good news, I think." Rose bit her lower lip and watched her husband's face closely. "Alec hasn't changed his offer financially but–"

Thomas closed his eyes.

"He wants us to stay."

"Stay?" Thomas frowned at her.

"And run the place. He said that *Heart of the Hills* simply wouldn't be the same without the Goodwin family." Rose smiled tentatively.

"He wants us to stay?"

She nodded. Happy tears were biting at the back of her throat. "He'll buy us out, we can clear our debts, and then we'll stay on as managers..." Rose waved her free hand at their bedroom. "Living here for as long as we want to." She tilted her head to the side. "I mean, we won't make as much money as we used to. And it'll be a challenge to figure out how it'll work, but Thomas, I think we should consider it. This place is our home, and–"

"Ha!" Thomas let out a loud thunderclap of laughter and stepped back from her, slapping his hand on his thigh in an almost pantomime fashion. "Yes! Rose, the answer is yes. A million times yes!" He reached for her, grabbed her waist and, before she could yell at him to put her down, was swirling her round in the centre of the room, lifting her off the floor and grinning.

"Thomas, you old fool, you'll hurt yourself!" Rose was

patting his shoulders, laughing, when Thomas stumbled. He tried to steady himself but tripped on the rug beneath his feet, and in seconds the pair of them had ended up in a heap on the bed.

Brushing her hair from her eyes and still laughing so much that her sides were aching, Rose rolled away from him and stared up at the ceiling. Breathless, she reached for Thomas' hand. "Did you hurt yourself?" She asked, squeezing his fingers.

"Only a little." Thomas pushed himself up onto his elbows and looked at her. "It was worth it."

"So, we're doing it? We're staying?"

Thomas nodded, but then stopped and brushed his hands through his silvery hair. "*We?*"

He was looking into her eyes, and Rose felt her heart beat a little faster. "Thomas," she whispered, "I never wanted us to be apart. You're the one who left."

"Because I was a coward, Rose. Not because I stopped loving you." Sliding closer, Thomas put an arm around Rose's waist and rested his forehead against hers. "I will never stop loving you, Rose Goodwin. And I swear, I'll spend every day of the rest of my life trying to win back your trust. Trying to make you see that without you..." He swiped his hand across his eyes, but it was too late – tears were already falling. "That without you, I'm–"

Rose raised her index finger to her husband's lips. "Thomas?" she said, pressing gently.

"Yes?"

"Stop talking and kiss me?"

49
AMELIE

IN THE DOORWAY of the ranch house, Amelie looked towards the dance floor. Music was drifting up from where the band was playing, the food had nearly all been demolished, and Cat was twirling with Ethan and Ben. Despite no wedding actually taking place, the guests were having a lovely time but, before anyone could spot her and wave her over, Amelie slipped quietly down the steps and across the stepping stones that led to the pool.

There, twelve hours after sitting in that very spot and deciding to call off her wedding, she dangled her feet into the warm water and looked up at the sky. It was a deep velvet shade of purple staccato'd with stars and, although she kept picturing Jed's face when he said goodbye to her and bundled himself into a taxi for the airport, the image of him was slowly beginning to fade.

"Perfect night for a party." Skye's voice made her breath catch in her chest and she turned to see that – to her surprise

– he was wearing a smart blue suit, a crisp white shirt, and a thin black tie.

"Well, look at you. All dressed up." She smiled and patted the stone floor beside her, gesturing for him to take a seat. "Didn't anyone tell you the wedding was cancelled?"

Without hesitating, Skye kicked off his shoes, removed his socks and rolled his trouser legs up to his knees so that he could sit and dip his toes in the water. "Well, I was hiding in the woods. So, I guess I didn't get the memo." He adjusted his collar. "But do I scrub up okay?"

"Very much so," Amelie said. "Although I thought you were boycotting the proceedings?"

"Turns out, I didn't have to." Skye raised his eyebrows at her.

She didn't know how much he'd been told about what happened and wasn't sure how to even begin to explain the emotions swirling around in her head. Thankfully, he spoke first.

"It was pretty brave, what you did."

Amelie laced her fingers together in her lap. "Brave would have been admitting that I was having second thoughts weeks ago… you know, *before* all the guests turned up."

Skye smiled at her and tilted his head to one side. "Don't be so hard on yourself." Then he shrugged his shoulders and laughed a little. "I probably didn't help matters. I should have backed off–"

Amelie stopped him mid-sentence by putting her hand on his forearm. "No," she said, "You shouldn't."

The fairy lights from the veranda were twinkling in Skye's sea-green eyes. He put his hand on top of hers.

"Skye..." She didn't know what she wanted to say, but before she could say anything, the music changed. Amelie smiled. "Do you remember this song? We loved it when we were kids."

Skye narrowed his eyes as he concentrated on making out the melody. His lips spread into a grin. "Yeah," he said. "I remember." Then, without warning, he stood up and extended his hand. "Come on, you've got to have a dance on your wedding day."

"It's not my wedding day. That's kind of the point. An *un*-wedding day, maybe." But she stood up anyway and let Skye put his hands on her waist.

For a few long minutes, they swayed back and forth to the music. Skye lifted his arm and twirled her around, then pulled her back into his chest with a flourish. "Have my dance moves improved since we were teenagers?"

"Oh, definitely," Amelie laughed, looking down at their bare feet and damp legs. But when she looked up, the song came to an end, and the music stopped. "The band must be packing up," she said quietly, suddenly unable to look away from him.

Skye's hands were still on her waist and, with her heart beating so fast she was certain he must be able to hear it, Amelie gently looped her arms around his neck. He stopped swaying. He brushed the side of her face with his fingertips, and Amelie let her eyes close. All thoughts of the wedding and the guests and Jed melted away from her.

Skye's lips were close to her ear. She could feel the warmth of his breath on her neck. "Just so you know," he whispered, "I will kiss you one day, Amelie Goodwin... but not today." Stepping back to meet her eyes, he smiled – an almost-cheeky, twinkling smile that dimpled his cheek. "Because the day I kiss you? Well, that will be the day I tell you I'm falling in love with you. And you can't tell a girl that kind of thing on her *un*-wedding day."

"No," she said, slipping her hand into his. "I don't suppose you can. But Skye?"

"Mmm?"

"I'm looking forward to it already."

EPILOGUE

Cat

CAT GOODWIN quietly closed her bedroom door and leaned against it. Her head was fuzzy with the unexpected joy of what should have been her sister's wedding day but had turned out to be simply a pretty good party. And her clothes were wet.

To everyone's surprise, and elation, Alec Anderson had agreed to keep her parents, and anyone else who wanted to stay on at the ranch. And when Mum and Dad had broken the news to them, some time after midnight as the guests piled into taxis to travel back to their B&Bs, the Goodwin kids – and Skye – had bolted down to the pool and hurled themselves into it fully clothed.

As she and Amelie came up for air, laughing and splashing huge armfuls of water at one another, Cat had shouted, "At least this time, you didn't push me!" and from the side of the pool, their mother had called, "What's all this about pushing? No one will tell me!"

With the memory bubbling away inside her, making her feel warm despite the dampness of her hair and skin, Cat padded over to her dressing table and sat down in front of the mirror.

Peering at herself, she swept her hands over her cheeks and examined her eyes. Although Amelie was adopted too, she and the twins had the same eyes – a light greyish blue. But Cat's had always been different – a deep hazel colour that, with her thick dark hair, made her look unmistakably Italian.

On the wall above the mirror, a picture of her family when they were all much younger was displayed proudly in a strong black frame. Cat stood up to look at it.

For the foreseeable future, the ranch would remain their home. The thought of it filled her with a giddy kind of happiness. But somewhere beneath the surface, something else was niggling at her.

It had started the summer before their father's accident – the day the adoption agency that had placed her with her parents had written to her and enclosed an envelope.

Miss Goodwin,
We have received correspondence from your birth mother.
She wishes to make contact with you. Enclosed is her letter.
You are under no obligation to read it, or to respond, and we
have not shared your name or address.

Your details remain confidential, unless you decide otherwise.

At first, Cat had scoffed and thrown both the letter and the envelope in the bin. The letter had been addressed to her, care of her parents, and they had watched her with wide, worried eyes as she opened it.

"Are you sure you don't want to read the other letter?" Mum had asked.

"Why would I?" Cat had replied.

But instead of smiling and helping her burn the letter, Mum had fished it out of the rubbish and – a few days later – had slipped it back into her hand. "You might change your mind one day. And if you do, that's okay."

Since then, Cat had kept it at the bottom of a suitcase in her apartment above the gelato store. When she moved back to the ranch, she'd brought it with her. And now here it was, tucked behind a photograph of the only family she'd ever really known, with its sharp white corner sticking out and begging her to touch it.

Shaking her head, Cat turned away.

But then she stopped. By her sides, her fingers twitched nervously.

All their lives, Amelie had seemed perfectly content with not knowing anything about her life before the ranch or about her biological parents. Each girl remembered snippets, most of them ugly and bleak, but while Cat had a nagging need to know more, Amelie was the opposite.

For years, Cat had ignored the feeling. She had pushed

away thoughts about what her birth mother was doing and where she was. She had refused to wonder whether she had brothers or sisters somewhere that she didn't know about.

But something had changed when she and Amelie argued by the pool that night, and it had been solidified when she finally – and tearfully – broke up with Filippo. For whatever reason, Cat knew that she wouldn't be truly content unless her questions were answered.

So, she slid the crumpled envelope from its hiding place, and she opened it.

Thank you for reading *A Heart Full of Secrets*, Book One in the *Heart of the Hills* series.

Book Two, *A Heart Full of Memories,* is available now.

So, if you want to catch up with Amelie and Skye's blossoming relationship, follow Cat on her own journey of self-discovery, and find out how Skye handles a ghost from his past, you can order your copy here.

You can also sign up to my mailing list at

poppypennington.com and will receive a free short story:
Love in the Alps.

And if you're longing to find out more about the Goodwin
family, why not travel back to the beginning with Rose and
Thomas' love story?
Love in Tuscany is available now.

THANK YOU!

Thank you so much for reading *A Heart Full of Secrets*. It's hard for me to say just how much I appreciate my readers. Especially those who get in touch. Please always feel free to email me at poppy@poppypennington.com.

If you enjoyed this book, please consider taking a moment to leave a review on Amazon.

To stay tuned about future releases, and receive the free short story *Love in the Alps,* sign up for my newsletter at: www.poppypennington.com

You can also follow me at:

- amazon.com/author/poppypenningtonsmith
- goodreads.com/Poppy_Pennington_Smith
- facebook.com/PoppyPennAuthor
- instagram.com/poppy_penn
- bookbub.com/authors/poppy-pennington-smith

ABOUT POPPY

Poppy Pennington-Smith writes atmospheric, wholesome romance novels and women's fiction.

Poppy has always been a romantic at heart. A sucker for a happy ending, she loves writing books that give you a warm, fuzzy feeling.

When she's not running around after Mr. P and Mini P, Poppy can be found drinking coffee from a Frida Kahlo mug, cuddled up in a mustard yellow blanket, and watching the garden from her writing shed.

Poppy's dream-come-true is talking to readers who enjoy her books. So, please do let her know what you think of them.

You can email poppy@poppypennington.com or join the PoppyPennReaders group on Facebook to get in touch.

You can also visit www.poppypennington.com.

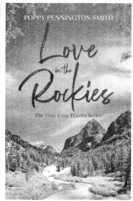

All of Poppy's books are free to read with Kindle Unlimited

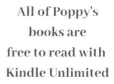

Printed in Great Britain
by Amazon

86508256R00171